Double Indemnity

James M. Cain (1892–1977) was born in Annapolis, Maryland and served in the US Army in World War 1. He worked as a journalist in Baltimore and New York in the 1920s, and spent the 1930s and 1940s as a screenwriter. His novels include *The Postman Always Rings Twice* (1934), *Serenade* (1937) and *Mildred Pierce* (1941).

Also by James M. Cain

crime**masterworks**

James M. Cain

Double Indemnity

TED SMART

This edition published in Great Britain in 2002 by Orion Books
an imprint of The Orion Publishing Group
Orion House, 5 Upper St Martin's Lane, London WC2H 9EA

This edition produced for
The Book People Ltd
Hall Wood Avenue,
Haydock,
St Helens WA11 9UL

A CIP catalogue record for this book
is available from the British Library

ISBN 0 75285 249 3 (cased)
ISBN 0 75284 769 4 (paperback)

Typeset by Deltatype Ltd, Birkenhead, Merseyside

Printed and bound in Great Britain by
Clays Ltd, St Ives plc

I drove out to Glendale to put three new truck drivers on a brewery company bond, and then I remembered this renewal over in Hollywoodland. I decided to run over there. That was how I came to this House of Death, that you've been reading about in the papers. It didn't look like a House of Death when I saw it. It was just a Spanish house, like all the rest of them in California, with white walls, red tile roof, and a patio out to one side. It was built cock-eyed. The garage was under the house, the first floor was over that, and the rest of it was spilled up the hill any way they could get it in. You climbed some stone steps to the front door, so I parked the car and went up there. A servant poked her head out. 'Is Mr Nirdlinger in?'

'I don't know, sir. Who wants to see him?'

'Mr Huff.'

'And what's the business?'

'Personal.'

Getting in is the tough part of my job, and you don't tip what you came for till you get where it counts. 'I'm sorry, sir, but they won't let me ask anybody in unless they say what they want.'

It was one of those spots you get in. If I said some more about 'personal' I would be making a mystery of it, and that's bad. If I said what I really wanted, I would be laying myself open for what every insurance agent dreads, that she would come back and say, 'Not in.' If I said I'd wait, I would be making myself look small, and that never helped a sale yet. To move this stuff, you've got to get in. Once you're in, they've got to listen to you, and you can pretty near rate an agent by how quick he gets to the family sofa, with his hat on one side of him and his dope sheets on the other.

'I see. I told Mr Nirdlinger I would drop in, but – never mind. I'll see if I can make it some other time.'

It was true, in a way. On this automobile stuff, you always make it a point that you'll give a reminder on renewal, but I hadn't seen him for a year. I made it sound like an old friend, though, and an old friend that wasn't any too pleased at the welcome he got. It worked. She got a worried look on her face. 'Well – come in, please.'

If I had used that juice trying to keep out, that might have got me somewhere.

I pitched my hat on the sofa. They've made a lot of that living room, especially those 'blood-red drapes.' All I saw was a living room like every other living room in California, maybe a little more expensive than some, but nothing that any department store wouldn't deliver on one truck, lay out in the morning, and have the credit OK ready the same afternoon. The furniture was Spanish, the kind that looks pretty and sits stiff. The rug was one of those 12 x 15's that would have been Mexican except it was made in Oakland, California. The blood-red drapes were there, but they didn't mean anything. All these Spanish houses have red velvet drapes that run on iron spears, and generally some red velvet wall tapestries to go with them. This was right out of the same can, with a coat-of-arms tapestry over the fireplace and a castle tapestry over the sofa. The other two sides of the room were windows and the entrance to the hall.

'Yes?'

A woman was standing there. I had never seen her before. She was maybe thirty-one or two, with a sweet face, light blue eyes, and dusty blonde hair. She was small, and had on a suit of blue house pajamas. She had a washed-out look.

'I wanted to see Mr Nirdlinger.'

'Mr Nirdlinger isn't in just now, but I am Mrs Nirdlinger. Is there something I could do?'

There was nothing to do but spill it. 'Why no, I think not, Mrs Nirdlinger, thanks just the same. Huff is my name, Walter Huff, of the General Fidelity of California. Mr Nirdlinger's automobile coverage runs out in a week or two, and I promised to give him a reminder on it, so I thought I'd drop by. But I certainly didn't mean to bother you about it.'

'Coverage?'

'Insurance. I just took a chance, coming up here in the daytime, but I happened to be in the neighborhood, so I thought it wouldn't hurt. When do you think would be a good time to see Mr Nirdlinger? Could he give me a few minutes right after dinner, do you think, so I wouldn't cut into his evening?'

'What kind of insurance has he been carrying? I ought to know, but I don't keep track.'

'I guess none of us keep track until something happens. Just the usual line. Collision, fire, and theft, and public liability.'

'Oh yes, of course.'

'It's only a routine matter, but he ought to attend to it in time, so he'll be protected.'

'It really isn't up to me, but I know he's been thinking about the Automobile Club. Their insurance, I mean.'

'Is he a member?'

'No, he's not. He's always intended to join, but somehow he's never got around to it. But the club representative was here, and he mentioned insurance.'

'You can't do better than the Automobile Club. They're prompt, liberal in their view of claims, and courteous straight down the line. I've not got a word to say against them.'

That's one thing you learn. Never knock the other guy's stuff.

'And then it's cheaper.'

'For members.'

'I thought only members could get it.'

'What I mean is this. If a man's going to join the Automobile Club anyway, for service in time of trouble, taking care of tickets, things like that, then if he takes their insurance too, he gets it cheaper. He certainly does. But if he's going to join the club just to get the insurance, by the time he adds that $16 membership fee to the premium rate, he's paying more. Figure that in, I can still save Mr Nirdlinger quite a little money.'

She talked along, and there was nothing I could do but

go along with it. But you sell as many people as I do, you don't go by what they say. You feel it, how the deal is going. And after a while I knew this woman didn't care anything about the Automobile Club. Maybe the husband did, but she didn't. There was something else, and this was nothing but a stall. I figured it would be some kind of a proposition to split the commission, maybe so she could get a ten-spot out of it without the husband knowing. There's plenty of that going on. And I was just wondering what I would say to her. A reputable agent don't get mixed up in stuff like that, but she was walking around the room, and I saw something I hadn't noticed before. Under those blue pajamas was a shape to set a man nuts, and how good I was going to sound when I started explaining the high ethics of the insurance business I didn't exactly know.

But all of a sudden she looked at me, and I felt a chill creep straight up my back and into the roots of my hair. 'Do you handle accident insurance?'

Maybe that don't mean to you what it meant to me. Well, in the first place, accident insurance is sold, not bought. You get calls for other kinds, for fire, for burglary, even for life, but never for accident. That stuff moves when agents move it, and it sounds funny to be asked about it. In the second place, when there's dirty work going on, accident is the first thing they think of. Dollar for dollar paid down, there's a bigger face coverage on accident than any other kind. And it's the one kind of insurance that can be taken out without the insured knowing a thing about it. No physical examination for accident. On that, all they want is the money, and there's many a man walking around today that's worth more to his loved ones dead than alive, only he don't know it yet.

'We handle all kinds of insurance.'

She switched back to the Automobile Club, and I tried to keep my eyes off her, and couldn't. Then she sat down. 'Would you like me to talk to Mr Nirdlinger about this, Mr Huff?'

Why would she talk to him about his insurance, instead of letting me do it? 'That would be fine, Mrs Nirdlinger.'

'It would save time.'

'Time's important. He ought to attend to this at once.'

But then she crossed me up. 'After he and I have talked it over, then you can see him. Could you make it tomorrow night? Say seven-thirty? We'll be through dinner by then.'

'Tomorrow night will be fine.'

'I'll expect you.'

I got in the car bawling myself out for being a fool just because a woman had given me one sidelong look. When I got back to the office I found Keyes had been looking for me. Keyes is head of the Claim Department, and the most tiresome man to do business with in the whole world. You can't even say today is Tuesday without he has to look on the calendar, and then check if it's this year's calendar or last year's calendar, and then find out what company printed the calendar, and then find out if their calendar checks with the World Almanac calendar. That amount of useless work you'd think would keep down his weight, but it don't. He gets fatter every year, and more peevish, and he's always in some kind of a feud with other departments of the company, and does nothing but sit with his collar open, and sweat, and quarrel, and argue, until your head begins spinning around just to be in the same room with him. But he's a wolf on a phoney claim.

When I got in there he got up and began to roar. It was a truck policy I had written about six months before, and the fellow had burned his truck up and tried to collect. I cut in on him pretty quick.

'What are you beefing to me for? I remember that case. And I distinctly remember that I clipped a memo to that application when I sent it through that I thought that fellow ought to be thoroughly investigated before we accepted the risk. I didn't like his looks, and I won't—'

'Walter, I'm not beefing to you. I know you said he ought to be investigated. I've got your memo right here on my desk. That's what I wanted to tell you. If other departments in this company would show half the sense that you show—'

'Oh.'

That would be like Keyes, that even when he wanted to say something nice to you, he had to make you sore first.

'And get this, Walter. Even after they issued the policy, in plain disregard of the warning on your memo, and even with that warning still looking them in the face, day before yesterday when the truck burned – they'd have paid that claim if I hadn't sent a tow car up there this afternoon, pulled the truck out, and found a pile of shavings under the engine, that proved it up on him that he started the fire himself.'

'Have you got him?'

'Oh, he confessed. He's taking a plea tomorrow morning, and that ends it. But my point is, that if you, just by looking at that man, could have your suspicions, why couldn't they—! Oh well, what's the use? I just wanted you to know it. I'm sending a memo to Norton about it. I think the whole thing is something the president of this company might very well look into. Though if you ask me, if the president of this company had more . . .'

He stopped and I didn't jog him. Keyes was one of the holdovers from the time of Old Man Norton, the founder of the company, and he didn't think much of young Norton, that took over the job when his father died. The way he told it, young Norton never did anything right, and the whole place was always worried for fear he'd pull them in on the feud. If young Norton was the man we had to do business with, then he was the man we had to do business with, and there was no sense letting Keyes get us in dutch with him. I gave Keyes's crack a dead pan. I didn't even know what he was talking about.

When I got back to my office, Nettie, my secretary, was just leaving. 'Goodnight, Mr Huff.'

'Goodnight, Nettie.'

'Oh – I put a memo on your desk, about a Mrs Nirdlinger. She called, about ten minutes ago, and said it would be inconvenient for you to call tomorrow night about that renewal. She said she'd let you know when to come.'

'Oh, thanks.'

She went, and I stood there, looking down at the

memo. It crossed my mind what kind of warning I was going to clip to *that* application, if, as, and when I got it.

  If any.

Three days later she called and left word I was to come at three-thirty. She let me in herself. She didn't have on the blue pajamas this time. She had on a white sailor suit, with a blouse that pulled tight over her hips, and white shoes and stockings. I wasn't the only one that knew about that shape. She knew about it herself, plenty. We went in the living room, and a tray was on the table. 'Belle is off today, and I'm making myself some tea. Will you join me?'

'Thank you, no, Mrs Nirdlinger. I'll only be a minute. That is, if Mr Nirdlinger has decided to renew. I supposed he had, when you sent for me.' Because it came over me that I wasn't surprised that Belle was off, and that she was just making herself some tea. And I meant to get out of there, whether I took the renewals with me or not.

'Oh, have some tea. I like tea. It makes a break in the afternoon.'

'You must be English.'

'No, native Californian.'

'You don't see many of them.'

'Most Californians were born in Iowa.'

'I was myself.'

'Think of that.'

The white sailor suit did it. I sat down. 'Lemon?'

'No thanks.'

'Two?'

'No sugar, just straight.'

'No sweet tooth?'

She smiled at me and I could see her teeth. They were big and white and maybe a little bit buck.

'I do a lot of business with the Chinese. They've got me out of the American way of drinking tea.'

'I love the Chinese. Whenever I make chow mein I buy all the stuff at the same place near the park. Mr Ling. Do you know him?'

'Known him for years.'

'Oh, you *have*!'

Her brow wrinkled up, and I saw there was nothing washed-out about her. What gave her that look was a spray of freckles across her forehead. She saw me looking at them. 'I believe you're looking at my freckles.'

'Yes, I was. I like them.'

'I don't.'

'I do.'

'I always used to wear a turban around my forehead when I went out in the sun, but so many people began stopping by, asking to have their fortunes told, that I had to stop it.'

'You don't tell fortunes?'

'No, it's one California accomplishment I never learned.'

'Anyway I like the freckles.'

She sat down beside me and we talked about Mr Ling. Now Mr Ling wasn't anybody but a Chinese grocery dealer that had a City Hall job on the side, and every year we had to bond him for $2,500, but you'd be surprised what a swell guy he turned out to be when we talked about him. After a while, though, I switched to insurance. 'Well, how about those policies?'

'He's still talking about the Automobile Club, but I think he's going to renew with you.'

'I'm glad of that.'

She sat there a minute, making little pleats with the edge of her blouse and rubbing them out. 'I didn't say anything to him about the accident insurance.'

'No?'

'I hate to talk to him about it.'

'I can understand that.'

'It seems an awful thing to tell him you think he ought to have an accident policy. And yet – you see, my husband is the Los Angeles representative of the Western Pipe and Supply Company.'

'He's in the Petroleum Building, isn't he?'

'That's where he has his office. But most of the time he's in the oilfields.'

'Plenty dangerous, knocking around there.'

'It makes me positively ill to think about it.'

'Does his company carry anything on him?'

'Not that I know of.'

'Man in a business like that, he ought not to take chances.'

And then I made up my mind that even if I did like her freckles, I was going to find out where I was at. 'I tell you, how would you like it if I talked with Mr

Nirdlinger about this? You know, not say anything about where I got the idea, but just bring it up when I see him.'

'I just *hate* to talk to him about it.'

'I'm telling you. *I'll* talk.'

'But then he'll ask me what I think, and – I won't know what to say. It's got me worried sick.'

She made another bunch of pleats. Then, after a long time, here it came. 'Mr Huff, would it be possible for me to take out a policy *for* him, without bothering him about it at all? I have a little allowance of my own. I could pay you for it, and he wouldn't know, but just the same all this worry would be over.'

I couldn't be mistaken about what she meant, not after fifteen years in the insurance business. I mashed out my cigarette, so I could get up and go. I was going to get out of there, and drop those renewals and everything else about her like a red-hot poker. But I didn't do it. She looked at me, a little surprised, and her face was about six inches away. What I did do was put my arm around her, pull her face up against mine, and kiss her on the mouth, hard. I was trembling like a leaf. She gave it a cold stare, and then she closed her eyes, pulled me to her, and kissed back.

'I liked you all the time.'

'I don't believe it.'

'Didn't I ask you to tea? Didn't I have you come here when Belle was off? I liked you the very first minute. I loved it, the solemn way you kept talking about your company, and all this and that. That was why I kept teasing you about the Automobile Club.'

'Oh, it was.'

'Now you know.'

I rumpled her hair, and then we both made some pleats in the blouse. 'You don't make them even, Mr Huff.'

'Isn't that even?'

'The bottom ones are bigger than the top. You've got to take just so much material every time, then turn it, then crease it, and then they make nice pleats. See?'

'I'll try to get the hang of it.'

'Not now. You've got to go.'

'I'm seeing you soon?'

'Maybe.'

'Well listen, I *am*.'

'Belle isn't off every day. I'll let you know.'

'Well – *will* you?'

'But don't *you* call *me* up. I'll let you know. I promise.'

'All right then. Kiss me good-bye.'

'Good-bye.'

I live in a bungalow in the Los Feliz hills. Daytime, I keep a Filipino house boy, but he don't sleep there. It was raining that night, so I didn't go out. I lit a fire and sat there, trying to figure out where I was at. I knew where I was at, of course. I was standing right on the deep end, looking over the edge, and I kept telling myself to get out of there, and get quick, and never come back. But that was what I kept telling myself. What I was doing was peeping over that edge, and all the time I was trying to pull away from it, there was something in me that kept edging a little closer, trying to get a better look.

A little before nine the bell rang. I knew who it was as soon as I heard it. She was standing there in a raincoat and a little rubber swimming cap, with the raindrops shining over her freckles. When I got her peeled off she was in sweater and slacks, just a dumb Hollywood outfit, but it looked different on her. I brought her to the fire and she sat down. I sat down beside her.

'How did you get my address?' It jumped out at me, even then, that I didn't want her calling my office asking questions about me.

'Phone book.'

'Oh.'

'Surprised?'

'No.'

'Well I like that. I never heard such conceit.'

'Your husband out?'

'Long Beach. They're putting down a new well. Three shifts. He had to go down. So I hopped on a bus. I think you might say you're glad to see me.'

'Great place, Long Beach.'

'I told Lola I was going to a picture show.'

'Who's Lola?'

'My stepdaughter.'

'Young?'

'Nineteen. Well, *are* you glad to see me?'

'Yeah, sure. Why – wasn't I expecting you?'

We talked about how wet it was out, and how we hoped it didn't turn into a flood, like it did the night before New Year's, 1934, and how I would run her back in the car. Then she looked in the fire a while. 'I lost my head this afternoon.'

'Not much.'

'A little.'

'You sorry?'

'– A little. I've never done that before. Since I've been married. That's why I came down.'

'You act like something really happened.'

'Something did. I lost my head. Isn't that something?'

'Well – so what?'

'I just wanted to say—'

'You didn't mean it.'

'No. I did mean it. If I hadn't meant it I wouldn't have had to come down. But I do want to say that I won't ever mean it again.'

'You sure?'

'Quite sure.'

'We ought to try and see.'

'No – please ... You see, I love my husband. More, here lately, than ever.'

I looked into the fire a while then. I ought to quit, while the quitting was good, I knew that. But that thing was in me, pushing me still closer to the edge. And then I could feel it again, that she wasn't saying what she meant. It was the same as it was that first afternoon I met her, that there was something else, besides what she was telling me. And I couldn't shake it off, that I had to call it on her.

'Why "here lately"?'

'Oh – worry.'

'You mean that down in the oilfields, some rainy night, a crown block is going to fall on him?'

'Please don't talk like that.'

'But that's the idea.'

'Yes.'

'I can understand that. Especially with this set-up.'

'. . . I don't quite know what you mean. What set-up?'

'Why – a crown block will.'

'Will what?'

'Fall on him.'

'Please, Mr Huff, I asked you not to talk like that. It's not a laughing matter. It's got me worried sick . . . What makes you say that?'

'*You're* going to drop a crown block *on* him.'

'I – *what!*'

'Well, you know, maybe not a crown block. But something. Something that's accidentally-on-purpose going to fall on him, and then he'll be dead.'

It nailed her between the eyes and they flickered. It was a minute before she said anything. She had to put on an act, and she was caught by surprise, and she didn't know how to do it.

'Are you – joking?'

'No.'

'You must be. Or you must be crazy. Why – I never heard of such a thing in my life.'

'I'm not crazy, and I'm not joking, and you've heard of such a thing in your life, because it's all you've thought of since you met me, and it's what you came down here for tonight.'

'I'll not stay here and listen to such things.'

'OK.'

'I'm going.'

'OK.'

'I'm going this minute.'
'OK.'

So I ran away from the edge, didn't I, and socked it into
her so she knew what I meant, and left it so we could
never go back to it again? I did not. That was what I
tried to do. I never even got up when she left, I didn't
help her on with her things, I didn't drive her back, I
treated her like I would treat an alley cat. But all the time
I knew it would be still raining the next night, that they
would still be drilling at Long Beach, that I would light
the fire and sit by it, that a little before nine the doorbell
would ring. She didn't even speak to me when she came
in. We sat by the fire at least five minutes before either
one of us said anything. Then she started it. 'How could
you say such things as you said to me last night?'

'Because they're true. That's what you're going to do.'

'*Now?* After what you've said?'

'Yes, after what I've said.'

'But – Walter, that's what I've come for, again,
tonight. I've thought it over. I realize that there have
been one or two things I've said that could give you a
completely wrong impression. In a way, I'm glad you
warned me about them, because I might have said them
to somebody else without knowing the – construction
that could be put upon them. But now that I do know,
you must surely see that – anything of that sort must be
out of my mind. Forever.'

That meant she had spent the whole day sweating
blood for fear I would warn the husband, or start
something, somehow. I kept on with it. 'You called me
Walter. What's your name?'

'Phyllis.'

'Phyllis, you seem to think that because I can call it on you, you're not going to do it. You *are* going to do it, and I'm going to help you.'

'*You!*'

'I.'

I caught her by surprise again, but she didn't even try to put on an act this time. 'Why – I couldn't have anybody help me! It would be – impossible.'

'You couldn't have anybody help you? Well let me tell you something. You had better have somebody help you. It would be nice to pull it off yourself, all alone, so nobody knew anything about it, it sure would. The only trouble with that is, you can't. Not if you're going up against an insurance company, you can't. You've got to have help. And it had better be help that knows its stuff.'

'What would you do this for?'

'You, for one thing.'

'What else?'

'Money.'

'You mean you would – betray your company, and help me do this, for me, and the money we could get out of it?'

'I mean just that. And you better say what you mean, because when I start, I'm going to put it through, straight down the line, and there won't be any slips. But I've got to know. Where I stand. You can't fool – with this.'

She closed her eyes, and after a while she began to cry. I put my arm around her and patted her. It seemed funny, after what we had been talking about, that I was treating her like some child that had lost a penny.

'Please, Walter, don't let me do this. We can't. It's simply – insane.'

'Yes, it's insane.'

'We're going to do it. I can feel it.'

'I too.'

'I haven't any reason. He treats me as well as a man can treat a woman. I don't love him, but he's never done anything to me.'

'But you're going to do it.'

'Yes, God help me, I'm going to do it.'

She stopped crying, and lay in my arms for a while without saying anything. Then she began to talk almost in a whisper.

'He's not happy. He'll be better off – dead.'

'Yeah?'

'That's not true, is it?'

'Not from where he sits, I don't think.'

'I know it's not true. I tell myself it's not true. But there's something in me, I don't know what. Maybe I'm crazy. But there's something in me that loves Death. I think of myself as Death, sometimes. In a scarlet shroud, floating through the night. I'm so beautiful, then. And sad. And hungry to make the whole world happy, by taking them out where I am, into the night, away from all trouble, all unhappiness ... Walter, this is the awful part. I know this is terrible. I tell myself it's terrible. But to me, it doesn't *seem* terrible. It seems as though I'm doing something – that's really best for him, if he only knew it. Do you understand me, Walter?'

'No.'

'Nobody could.'

'But we're going to do it.'

'Yes, we're going to do it.'

'Straight down the line.'

'Straight down the line.'

A night or two later, we talked about it just as casually as if it was a little trip to the mountains. I had to find out what she had been figuring on, and whether she had gummed it up with some bad move of her own. 'Have you said anything to him about this, Phyllis? About this policy?'

'No.'

'Absolutely nothing?'

'Not a thing.'

'All right, how are you going to do it?'

'I was going to take out the policy first—'

'Without him knowing?'

'Yes.'

'Holy smoke, they'd have crucified you. It's the first thing they look for. Well – anyway that's out. What else?'

'He's going to build a swimming pool. In the spring. Out in the patio.'

'And?'

'I thought it could be made to look as though he hit his head diving or something.'

'That's out. That's still worse.'

'Why? People do, don't they?'

'It's no good. In the first place, some fool in the insurance business, five or six years ago, put out a newspaper story that most accidents happen in people's own bathtubs, and since then bathtubs, swimming pools, and fishponds are the first thing they think of. When they're trying to pull something, I mean. There's two cases like that out here in California right now. Neither one of them are on the up-and-up, and if there'd been an insurance angle those people would wind up on the gallows. Then it's a daytime job, and you never can tell who's peeping at you from the next hill. Then a swimming pool is like a tennis court, you no sooner have one than it's a community affair, and you don't know who might come popping in on you at any minute. And then it's one of those things where you've got to watch for your chance, and you can't plan it in advance, and know where you're going to come out to the last decimal point. Get this, Phyllis. There's three essential elements to a successful murder.'

That word was out before I knew it. I looked at her quick. I thought she'd wince under it. She didn't. She leaned forward. The firelight was reflected in her eyes like she was some kind of leopard. 'Go on. I'm listening.'

'The first is, help. One person can't get away with it, that is unless they're going to admit it and plead the unwritten law or something. It takes more than one. The second is, the time, the place, the way, all known in advance – to us, but not to him. The third is, audacity. That's the one that all amateur murderers forget. They know the first two, sometimes. But that third, only a professional knows. There comes a time in any murder when the only thing that can see you through is audacity, and I can't tell you why. You know the perfect murder? You think it's this swimming pool job, and you're going to do it so slick nobody would ever guess it. They'd guess it in two seconds, flat. In three seconds, flat, they'd prove it, and in four seconds, flat, you'd confess it. No, that's not it. The perfect murder is the gangster that goes on the spot. You know what they do? First they get a finger on him. They get that girl that he lives with. Along about six o'clock they get a phone call from her. She goes out to a drugstore to buy some lipstick, and she calls. They're going to see a picture tonight, he and she, and it's at such and such a theater. They'll get there around nine o'clock. All right, there's the first two elements. They got help, and they fixed the time and the place in advance. All right, now watch the third. They go there in a car. They park across the street. They keep the motor running. They put a sentry out. He loafs up an alley, and pretty soon he drops a handker-chief and picks it up. That means he's coming. They get out of the car. They drift up to the theater. They close in on him. And right there, in the glare of the lights, with a couple hundred people looking on, they let him have it. He hasn't got a chance. Twenty bullets hit him, from four or five automatics. He falls, they scram for the car, they drive off – and then you try to convict them. You just try to convict them. They've got their alibis ready in advance, all airtight, they were only seen for a second, by people who were so scared they didn't know what they were looking at – and there isn't a chance to convict them. The police know who they are, of course. They round them up, give them the water cure – and then they're habeas-corpused into court and turned loose. Those guys don't get convicted. They get put on the spot by other gangsters. Oh yeah, they know their stuff, all right. And if we want to get away with it, we've got to do it the way they do it, and not the way some punk up near San Francisco does it, that's had two trials already, and still he's not free.'

'Be bold?'

'Be bold. It's the only way.'

'If we shot him it wouldn't be accident.'

'That's right. We don't shoot him, but I want you to get the principle through your head. Be bold. It's the only chance to get away with it.'

'Then how—?'

'I'm coming to that. Another trouble with your swimming pool idea is that there's no money in it.'

'They'd have to pay –'

'They'd have to pay, but this is a question of how much they'd have to pay. All the big money on an accident policy comes from railroad accidents. They found out pretty quick, when they began to write accident insurance, that the apparent danger spots, the spots that people think are danger spots, aren't danger spots at all. I mean, people always think a railroad train is a pretty dangerous place to be, or they did, anyway, before the novelty wore off, but the figures show not many people get killed, or even hurt, on railroad trains. So on accident policies, they put in a feature that sounds pretty good to the man that buys it, because *he's* a little worried about train trips, but it doesn't cost the company much, because it knows he's pretty sure to get there safely. They pay double indemnity for railroad accidents. That's just where we cash in. You've been thinking about some piker job, maybe, and a fat chance I'd be taking a chance like this for that. When we get

24

done, we cash a $50,000 bet, and if we do it right, we're going to cash it, don't make any mistake about that.'

'Fifty thousand dollars?'

'Nice?'

'My!'

'Say, this is a beauty, if I do say it myself. I didn't spend all this time in this business for nothing, did I? Listen, he knows all about this policy, and yet he don't know a thing about it. He applies for it, in writing, and yet he don't apply for it. He pays me for it with his own check, and yet he don't pay me. He has an accident happen to him and yet he don't have an accident happen to him. He gets on the train, and yet he don't get on it.'

'What *are* you talking about?'

'You'll find out. The first thing is, we've got to fix him up with that policy. I sell it to him, do you get that? – except that I don't sell him. Not quite. I give him the works, the same as I give any other prospect. And I've got to have witnesses. Get that. There's got to be somebody that heard me go right after him. I show him that he's covered on everything that might hurt the automobile, but hasn't got a thing that covers personal injury to himself. I put it up to him whether a man isn't worth more than his car. I—'

'Suppose he buys?'

'Well – suppose he does? He won't. I can bring him within one inch of the line and hold him there, don't you think I can't. I'm a salesman, if I'm nothing else. But – I've got to have witnesses. Anyway, one witness.'

'I'll have somebody.'

'Maybe you better oppose it.'

'All right.'

'You're all for the automobile stuff, when I start in on that, but this accident thing gives you the shivers.'

'I'll remember.'

'You better make a date pretty quick. Give me a ring.'

'Tomorrow?'

'Confirm by phone. Remember, you need a witness.'

'I'll have one.'

'Tomorrow, then. Subject to call.'

'Walter – I'm so excited. It does terrible things to me.'

'I too.'

'Kiss me.'

You think I'm nuts? All right, maybe I am. But you spend fifteen years in the business I'm in, maybe you'll go nuts yourself. You think it's a business, don't you, just like your business, and maybe a little better than that, because it's the friend of the widow, the orphan, and the needy in time of trouble? It's not. It's the biggest gambling wheel in the world. It don't look like it, but it is, from the way they figure the percentage on the OO to the look on their face when they cash your chips. You bet that your house will burn down, they bet it won't, that's all. What fools you is that you didn't *want* your house to burn down when you made the bet, and so you forget it's a bet. That don't fool them. To them a bet is a bet, and a hedge bet don't look any different than any other bet. But there comes a time, maybe, when you *do* want your house to burn down, when the money is worth more than the house. And right there is where the trouble starts. They know there's just so many people out there that are out to crook that wheel, and that's when they get tough. They've got their spotters out there, they know every crooked trick there is, and if you

26

want to beat them you had better be good. So long as you're honest, they'll pay you with a smile, and you may even go home thinking it was all in a spirit of good clean fun. But you start something, and then you'll find out.

All right, I'm an agent. I'm a croupier in that game. I know all their tricks, I lie awake nights thinking up tricks, so I'll be ready for them when they come at me. And then one night I think up a trick, and get to thinking I could crook the wheel myself if I could only put a plant out there to put down my bet. That's all. When I met Phyllis I met my plant. If that seems funny to you, that I would kill a man just to pick up a stack of chips, it might not seem so funny if you were back of that wheel, instead of out front. I had seen so many houses burned down, so many cars wrecked, so many corpses with blue holes in their temples, so many awful things that people had pulled to crook the wheel, that that stuff didn't seem real to me any more. If you don't understand that, go to Monte Carlo or some other place where there's a big casino, sit at a table, and watch the face of the man that spins the little ivory balls. After you've watched it a while, ask yourself how much he would care if you went out and plugged yourself in the head. His eyes might drop when he heard the shot, but it wouldn't be from worry whether you lived or died. It would be to make sure you didn't leave a bet on the table, that he would have to cash for your estate. No, he wouldn't care. Not that baby.

3

'Then another thing I call your attention to, Mr Nirdlinger, a feature we've added in the last year, at no extra cost, is our guarantee of bail bond. We furnish you a card, and all you have to do, in case of accident where you're held responsible, or in any traffic case where the police put you under arrest, is to produce that card and if it's a bailable offense, it automatically procures your release. The police take up the card, that puts us on your bond, and you're free until your case comes up for trial. Since that's one of the things the Automobile Club does for members, and you're thinking about the Automobile Club—'

'I've pretty well given that idea up.'

'Well then, why don't we fix this thing up right now? I've pretty well outlined what we do for you—'

'I guess we might as well.'

'Then if you'll sign these applications, you'll be protected until the new policies are issued, which will be in about a week, but there's no use your paying for a whole week's extra insurance. There's for the collision, fire, and theft, there's for the public liability – and if you don't mind sticking your name on these two, they're the agent's copies, and I keep them for my files.'

'Here?'

'Right on the dotted line.'

He was a big, blocky man, about my size, with glasses, and I played him exactly the way I figured to. As soon as I had the applications, I switched to accident insurance. He didn't seem much interested, so I made it pretty stiff. Phyllis cut in that the very idea of accident insurance made her shiver, and I kept on going. I didn't quit till I had hammered in every reason for taking out accident insurance that any agent ever thought of, and maybe a couple of reasons that no agent ever had thought of. He sat there drumming with his fingers on the arms of his chair, wishing I would go.

But what bothered me wasn't that. It was the witness that Phyllis brought out. I thought she would have some friend of the family in to dinner, maybe a woman, and just let her stay with us, there in the sitting room, after I showed up around seven-thirty. She didn't. She brought the stepdaughter in, a pretty girl, named Lola. Lola wanted to go, but Phyllis said she had to get the wool wound for a sweater she was knitting, and kept her there, winding it. I had to tie her in, with a gag now and then, to make sure she would remember what we were talking about, but the more I looked at her the less I liked it. Having to sit with her there, knowing all the time what we were going to do to her father, was one of the things I hadn't bargained for.

And next thing I knew, when I got up to go, I had let myself in for hauling her down to the boulevard, so she could go to a picture show. Her father had to go out again that night, and he was using the car, and that meant that unless I hauled her she would have to go down by bus. I didn't want to haul her. I didn't want to have anything to do with her. But when he kind of turned to me there was nothing I could do but offer, and she ran and got her hat and coat, and in a minute or two there we were, rolling down the hill.

'Mr Huff?'

'Yes?'

'I'm not going to a picture show.'

'No?'

'I'm meeting somebody. At the drugstore.'

'Oh.'

'Would you haul us both down?'

'Oh – sure.'

'You won't mind?'

'No, not a bit.'

'And you won't tell on me? There are reasons why I don't want them to know. At home.'

'No, of course not.'

We stopped at the drugstore, and she jumped out and in a minute came back with a young guy, with an Italian-looking face, pretty good-looking, that had been standing around outside. 'Mr Huff, this is Mr Sachetti.'

'How are you, Mr Sachetti. Get in.'

They got in, and kind of grinned at each other, and we rolled down Beachwood to the boulevard. 'Where do you want me to set you down?'

'Oh, anywhere.'

'Hollywood and Vine all right?'

'Swell.'

I set them down there, and after she got out, she reached out her hand, and took mine, and thanked me, her eyes shining like stars. 'It was darling of you to take us. Lean close I'll tell you a secret.'

'Yes?'

'If you hadn't taken us we'd have had to walk.'

'How are you going to get back?'

'Walk.'

'You want some money?'

'No, my father would kill me. I spent all my week's money. No, but thanks. And remember – don't tell on me.'

'I won't.'

'Hurry, you'll miss your light.

I drove home. Phyllis got there in about a half hour. She was humming a song out of a Nelson Eddy picture. 'Did you like my sweater?'

'Yeah, sure.'

'Isn't it a lovely color? I never wore old rose before. I think it's going to be really becoming to me.'

'It's going to look all right.'

'Where did you leave Lola?'

'On the boulevard.'

'Where did she go?'

'I didn't notice.'

'Was there somebody waiting for her?'

'Not that I saw. Why?'

'I was just wondering. She's been going around with a boy named Sachetti. A perfectly terrible person. She's been forbidden to see him.'

'He wasn't on deck tonight. Anyway, I didn't see him. Why didn't you tell me about her?'

'Well? You said have a witness.'

'Yeah, but I didn't mean her.'

'Isn't she as good a witness as any other?'

'Yeah, but holy smoke there's a limit. A man's own daughter, and we're even using her – for what we're using her for.'

An awful look came over her face, and her voice got hard as glass. 'What's the matter? Are you getting ready to back out?'

'No, but you could have got somebody else. Me, driving her down to the boulevard, and all the time I had this in my pocket.' I took out the applications, and showed them to her. One of those 'agent's copies' was an undated application for a $25,000 personal accident policy, with double indemnity straight down the line for any disability or death incurred on a railroad train.

It was part of the play that I had to make two or three calls on Nirdlinger in his office. The first time, I gave him the bail-bond guarantee, stuck around about five minutes, told him to put it in his car, and left. The next time I gave him a little leather memo book, with his name stamped on it in gilt, just a little promotion feature we have for policy holders. The third time I delivered the automobile policies, and took his check, $79.52. When I got back to the office that day, Nettie told me there was somebody waiting for me in my private office. 'Who?'

'A Miss Lola Nirdlinger and a Mr Sachetti, I think she said. I didn't get his first name.'

I went in there and she laughed. She liked me, I could see that. 'You surprised to see us again?'

'Oh, not much. What can I do for you?'

'We've come in to ask a favor. But it's your own fault.'

'Yeah? How's that?'

'What you said the other night to Father about being able to get money on his car, if he needed it. We've come in to take you up on it. Or anyway, Nino has.'

That was something I had to do something about, the competition I was getting from the Automobile Club on an automobile loan. They lend money on a member's car, and I got to the point where I had to, too, if I was going to get any business. So I organized a little finance company of my own, had myself made a director, and spent about one day a week there. It didn't have anything to do with the insurance company, but it was one way I could meet that question that I ran into all the time: 'Do you lend money on a car?' I had mentioned it to Nirdlinger, just as part of the sales talk, but I didn't know she was paying attention. I looked at Sachetti. 'You want to borrow money on your car?'

'Yes sir.'

'What kind of car is it?'

He told me. It was a cheap make.

'Sedan?'

'Coupe.'

'It's in your name? And paid for?'

'Yes sir.'

They must have seen a look cross my face, because she giggled. 'He couldn't use it the other night. He didn't have any gas.'

'Oh.'

I didn't want to lend him money on his car, or

anything else. I didn't want to have anything to do with him, or her, in any way, shape, or form. I lit a cigarette, and sat there a minute. 'You sure you want to borrow money on this car? Because if you're not working now, what I mean if you don't absolutely see your way clear to pay it back, it's a sure way to lose it. The whole second-hand car business depends on people that thought they could pay a small loan back, and couldn't.'

She looked at me very solemnly. 'It's different with Nino. He isn't working, but he doesn't want this loan just to have money to spend. You see, he's done all his work for his Sc.D., and—'

'Where?'

'USC.'

'What in?'

'Chemistry. If he can only get his degree, he's sure of work, he's been promised that, and it seems such a pity to miss a chance for a really good position just because he hasn't taken his degree. But to take it, he has to have his dissertation published, and pay this and that, for his diploma for instance, and that's what he wants this money for. He won't spend it on his living. He has friends that will take care of that.'

I had to come through. I knew that. I wouldn't have, if it didn't make me so nervous to be around her, but all I could think of now was to say yes and get them out of there. 'How much do you want?'

'He thought if he could get $250, that would be enough.'

'I see. I see.'

I figured it up. With charges, it would amount to around $285, and it was an awfully big loan on the car he was going to put up. 'Well – give me a day or two on it. I think we can manage it.'

They went out, and then she ducked back. 'You're awfully nice to me. I don't know why I keep bothering you about things.'

'That's all right, Miss Nirdlinger, I'm glad—'

'You can call me Lola, if you want to.'

'Thanks, I'll be glad to help any time I can.'

'This is secret, too.'

'Yes, I know.'

'I'm terribly grateful, Mr Huff.'

'Thanks – Lola.'

The accident policy came through a couple of days later. That meant I had to get his check for it, and get it right away, so the dates would correspond. You understand, I wasn't going to deliver the accident policy, to him. That would go to Phyllis, and she would find it later, in his safe deposit box. And I wasn't going to tell him anything about it. Just the same, I had to get his check, in the exact amount of the policy, so later on, when they checked up his stubs and the cancelled checks, they would find he had paid for it himself. That would check with the application in our files, and it would also check with those trips I had made to his office, if they put me on the spot.

I went in on him pretty worried, and shut the door on his secretary, and got down to brass tacks right away. 'Mr Nirdlinger, I'm in a hole, and I'm wondering if you'll help me out.'

'Well I don't know. I don't know. What is it?'

He was expecting a touch, and I wanted him to be expecting a touch. 'It's pretty bad.'

'Suppose you tell me.'

'I've charged you too much for your insurance. For that automobile stuff.'

He burst out laughing. 'Is that all? I thought you wanted to borrow money.'

'Oh. No. Nothing like that. It's worse – from my point of view.'

'Do I get a refund?'

'Why sure.'

'Then it's better – from my point of view.'

'It isn't as simple as that. This is the trouble, Mr Nirdlinger. There's a board, in our business, that was formed to stop cut-throating on rates, and see to it that every company charges a rate sufficient to protect the policy holder, and that's the board I'm in dutch with. Because here recently, they've made it a rule that *every* case, every case, mind you, where there's an alleged mischarge by an agent, is to be investigated by them, and you can see where that puts me. And you too, in a way. Because they'll have me up for fifteen different hearings, and come around pestering you till you don't know what your name is – and all because I looked up the wrong rate in the book when I was out to your house that night, and never found it out till this morning when I checked over my month's accounts.'

'And what do you want to do?'

'There's one way I can fix it. Your check, of course, was deposited, and there's nothing to do about that. But if you'll let me give you cash for the check you gave me – $79.52 – I've got it right here with me – and give me a new check for the correct amount – $58.60 then that'll balance it, and they'll have nothing to investigate.'

'How do you mean, balance it?'

'Well, you see, in multiple-card bookkeeping – oh well, it's so complicated I don't even know if I understand it myself. Anyway, that's what our cashier tells me. It's the way they make their entries.'

'I see.'

He looked out the window and I saw a funny look come in his eye. 'Well – all right. I don't know why not.'

I gave him the cash and took his check. It was all hooey. We've got a board, but it doesn't bother with agents' mistakes. It governs rates. I don't even know if there's such a thing as multiple-card bookkeeping, and I never talked with our cashier. I just figured that when you offer a man about twenty bucks more than he thought he had when you came in, he wouldn't ask too many questions about why you offer it to him. I went to the bank. I deposited the check. I even knew what he wrote on his stub. It just said 'Insurance.' I had what I wanted.

It was the day after that that Lola and Sachetti came in for their loan. When I handed them the check she did a little dance in the middle of the floor. 'You want a copy of Nino's dissertation?'

'Why – I'd love it.'

'It's called "The Problem of Colloids in the Reduction of Low-Grade Gold Ores."'

'I'll look forward to it.'

'Liar – you won't even read it.'

'I'll read as much as I can understand.'
'Anyway, you'll get a signed copy.'
'Thanks.'
'Good-bye. Maybe you're rid of us for a while.'
'Maybe.'

4

All this, what I've been telling you, happened in late winter, along the middle of February. Of course, in California February looks like any other month, but anyway it would have been winter anywhere else. From then on, all through the spring, believe me I didn't get much sleep. You start on something like this, and if you don't wake up plenty of times in the middle of the night, dreaming they got you for something you forgot, you've got better nerves than I've got. Then there were things we couldn't figure out, like how to get him on a train. That was tough, and if we didn't have a piece of luck, maybe we never would have put it over. There's plenty of people out here that have never been inside a train, let alone taken a ride on one. They go everywhere by car. That was how he traveled, when he traveled, and how to make him use a train just once, that was something that gave us a headache for quite some time. We got a break on one thing though that I had sweated over plenty. That was the funny look that came over his face when I got that check. There was something back of it, I knew that, and if it was something his secretary was in on, and especially if he went out after I left and made some crack to the secretary about getting $20 he didn't expect, it would look plenty bad later, no matter what kind of story I made up. But that wasn't it. Phyllis got the low-down on it, and it startled me, how pretty it broke for us. He charged his car insurance to his company, under expenses, and his secretary had already entered it when I came along with my proposition. She had not only entered it, but if he went through with what I wanted, he still had his cancelled check to show for it, the first one, I mean. All he had to do was keep his mouth shut to the secretary and he could put his $20 profit in his pocket, and nobody would be the wiser. He kept his mouth shut. He didn't even tell Lola. But he had to brag to somebody how smart he was, so he told Phyllis.

Another thing that worried me was myself. I was afraid my work would fall off, and they'd begin talking about me in the office, wondering why I'd begun to slip. That wouldn't do me any good, later I mean, when they began to think about it. I had to sell insurance while this thing was cooking, if I never sold it before. I worked like a wild man. I saw every prospect there was the least chance of selling, and how I high-pressured them was a shame. Believe it or not, my business showed a 12% increase in March, it jumped 2% over that in April, and in May, when there's a lot of activity in cars, it went to 7% over that. I even made a hook-up with a big syndicate of second-hand dealers for my finance company, and that helped. The books didn't know anything to tell on me. I was the candy kid in both offices that spring. They were all taking off their hats to me.

*

'He's going to his class reunion. At Palo Alto.'

'When?'

'June. In about six weeks.'

'That's it. That's what we've been waiting for.'

'But he wants to drive. He wants to take the car, and he wants me to go with him. He'll raise an awful fuss if I don't go.'

'Yeah? Listen, don't give yourself airs. I don't care if it's a class reunion or just down to the drugstore, a man would rather go alone than with a wife. He's just being polite. You talk like you're not interested in his class reunion, and he'll be persuaded. He'll be persuaded so easy you'll be surprised.'

'Well I like that.'

'You're not supposed to like it. But you'll find out.'

That was how it turned out, but she worked on him a whole week and she couldn't change him on the car. 'He says he'll have to have it, and there'll be a lot of things he'll want to go to, picnics and things like that, and if he doesn't have it he'll have to hire one. Besides, he hates trains. He gets trainsick.'

'Can't you put on an act?'

'I did. I put on all the act I dare put, and still he won't budge. I put on such an act that Lola is hardly speaking to me any more. She thinks it's selfish of me. I can try again, but—'

'Holy smoke no.'

'I could do this. The day before he's to start, I could bang the car up. Mess up the ignition or something. So it had to go in the shop. Then he'd *have* to go by train.'

'Nothing like it. Nothing even a little bit like it. In the first place, if you've already put on an act, they'll smell something, and believe me Lola will be hard to talk down, later. In the second place, we need the car.'

'*We* need it?'

'It's essential.'

'I still don't know – what we're going to do.'

'You'll know. You'll know in plenty of time. But we've got to have the car. We've got to have two cars, yours and mine. Whatever you do, don't pull any monkey business with the car. That car's got to run. It's got to be in perfect shape.'

'Hadn't we better give up the train idea?'

'Listen, it's the train or we don't do it.'

'Well my goodness, you don't have to snap at me.'

'Just pulling off some piker job, that don't interest me. But this, hitting it for the limit, that's what I go for. It's all I go for.'

'I was just wondering.'

'Quit wondering.'

Two or three days later was when we had our piece of luck. She called me at the office around four in the afternoon. 'Walter?'

'Yes.'

'Are you alone?'

'Is it important?'

'Yes, terribly. Something has happened.'

'I'll go home. Call me there in a half hour.'

I was alone, but I don't take chances on a phone that runs through a switchboard. I went home, and the phone rang a couple of minutes after I got there. 'The Palo Alto trip is off. He's broken his leg.'

'What!'

'I don't even know how he did it, yet. He was holding a dog or something, a neighbor's dog that was chasing a rabbit, and slipped and fell down. He's in the hospital now. Lola's with him. They'll be bringing him home in a few minutes.'

'I guess that knocks it in the head.'

'I'm afraid so.'

I was at dinner before it came to me that instead of knocking it in the head, maybe this fixed it up perfect. I walked three miles, around the living room, wondering if she'd come that night, before I heard the bell ring.

'I've only got a few minutes. I'm supposed to be on the boulevard, buying him something to read. I could cry. Whoever heard of such a thing?'

'Listen, Phyllis, never mind that. What kind of break has he got? I mean, is it bad?'

'It's down near the ankle. No, it's not bad.'

'Is it in pulleys?'

'No. There's a weight on it, that comes off in about a week. But he won't be able to walk. He'll have to wear a cast. A long time.'

'He'll be able to walk.'

'You think so?'

'If you get him up.'

'What do you mean, Walter?'

'On crutches, he can get up, if you get him up. Because with his foot in a cast, *he won't be able to drive*. He'll have to go by train. Phyllis, this is what we've been hoping for.'

'You think so?'

'And then another thing. I told you, he gets on that

train but he don't get on it. All right, then. We've got a question of identication there, haven't we? Those crutches, that foot in a cast – there's the most perfect identification a man ever had. Oh yeah, I'm telling you. If you can get him off that bed, and make him think he ought to take the trip anyway, just as a vacation from all he's been through – we're in. I can feel it. We're in.'

'It's dangerous, though.'

'What's dangerous about it?'

'I mean, getting a broken leg case out of bed too soon. I used to be a nurse, and I know. It's almost certain to affect the length. Make one leg shorter than the other, I mean.'

'Is that all that's bothering you?'

It was a minute before she got it. Whether one leg was going to be shorter than the other, that was one thing he didn't have to worry about.

Decoration Day they don't have mail delivery, but the day watchman sends over to the General Fidelity box and gets it. There was a big envelope for me, marked personal. I opened it and found a booklet. It was called 'Colloids in Gold Mining. An examination of methods in dealing with the problem.' Inside, it was inscribed, 'To Mr Walter Huff, in appreciation of past favors, Bernanino Sachetti.'

5

His train was to leave at 9:45 at night. Around four o'clock, I drove down to San Pedro Street and talked employers' liability to the manager of a wine company. There wasn't a chance of landing him until August, when the grapes came in and his plant opened up, but I had a reason. He explained why he wasn't ready to do business yet, but I put on an act and went back to the office. I told Nettie I thought I had a real prospect, and to make out a card for him. The card automatically gave the date of the first call, and that was what I wanted. I signed a couple of letters, and around five-thirty I left.

I got home around six, and the Filipino was all ready to serve dinner. I had seen to that. This was June 3, and I should have paid him on the first, but I had pretended I had forgotten to go to the bank, and put him off. Today, though, I had stopped at the house for lunch, and paid him. That meant that when night came he could hardly wait to go out and spend it. I said OK, he could serve dinner, and he had the soup on the table before I even got washed up. I ate, as well as I could. He gave me steak, mashed potatoes, peas, and carrots, with fruit cup for dessert. I was so nervous I could hardly chew, but I got it all down somehow. I had hardly finished my coffee when he had everything washed up, and had changed to cream-colored pants, white shoes and stockings, a brown coat, and white shirt open at the neck, ready to go out with the girl. It used to be that what a Hollywood actor wore on Monday a Filipino house boy wore on Tuesday, but now, if you ask me, it's the other way around, and the boy from Manila beats Clark Gable to it.

He left around a quarter to seven. When he came up to ask if there was anything else for him to do, I was taking off my clothes getting ready to go to bed. I told him I was going to lie there and do a little work. I got some paper and pencils and made a lot of notes, like I was figuring up the public liability stuff for the man I talked to in the afternoon. It was the kind of stuff you would naturally save and put in the prospect's folder. I took care there was a couple of notes on the date.

Then I went down and called the office. Joe Pete, the night watchman, answered. 'Joe Pete, this is Walter Huff. Do me a favor, will you? Go up to my office, and right on top of the desk you'll find my rate book. It's a looseleaf book, with a soft leather back, and my name stamped in gold on the front, and under that the word 'rates.' I forgot to bring it home, and I need it. Will you get it and send it up to me by messenger, right away?'

'OK, Mr Huff. Right away.'

Fifteen minutes later he rang back and said he couldn't find it. 'I looked all over the desk, Mr Huff, and through the office besides, and there's no such book there.'

'Nettie must have locked it up.'

'I can call her if you want, and ask where she put it.'

'No, I don't need it that bad.'

'I'm sorry, Mr Huff.'

'I'll have to get along without it.'

I had put that rate book in a place where he'd never find it. But it was one person that had called me at home that night, and I was there, working hard. There'd be others. No need to say anything to him that would make him remember the date. He had to keep a log, and enter everything he did, not only by date, but also by time. I looked at my watch. It was 7:38.

A quarter to eight the phone rang again. It was Phyllis. 'The blue.'

'Blue it is.'

That was a check on what suit he would wear. We were pretty sure it would be the blue, but I had to be sure, so she was to duck down to the drugstore to buy him an extra tooth brush, and call. No danger of it being traced, there's no record on dial calls. Soon as she hung up I dressed. I put on a blue suit too. But before that I wrapped up my foot. I put a thick bandage of gauze on it, and over that adhesive tape. It looked like the tape was wrapped on the ankle, like a cast for a broken leg, but it wasn't. I could cut it off in ten seconds when I was ready to. I put the shoe on. I could barely lace it, but that was how I wanted it. I checked on a pair of horn-rim glasses, like he wore. They were in my pocket. So was 58 inches of light cotton rope, rolled small. So was a handle I had made, like stores hook on packages, but heavier, from an iron rod. My coat bulged, but I didn't care.

*

Twenty minutes to nine I called Nettie. 'Did you see my rate book before I left?'

'Indeed I didn't, Mr Huff.'

'I need it, and I don't know what I did with it.'

'You mean you lost it?'

'I don't know. I phoned Joe Pete, and he can't find it, and I can't imagine what I did with it.'

'I can run in, if you want, and see if I can—'

'No, it's not that important.'

'I didn't see it, Mr Huff.'

Nettie lives in Burbank, and it's a toll call. The record would show I called from the house at 8:40. As soon as I got rid of her I opened the bell box and tilted half a visiting card against the clapper, so if the phone rang it would fall down. Then I did the same for the doorbell clapper, in the kitchen. I would be out of the house an hour and a half, and I had to know if the doorbell rang or the phone rang. If they did, that would be while I was in the bathroom taking a bath, with the door shut and the water running, so I didn't hear. But I had to know.

Soon as I had the cards fixed I got in my car and drove over to Hollywoodland. It's just a few minutes from my house. I parked on the main street, a couple of minutes' walk from the house. I had to be where a car wouldn't attract any attention, but at the same time I couldn't be so far off that I had to do much walking. Not with that foot.

Around the bend from the house is a big tree. There's no house in sight of it. I slipped behind it and waited. I waited exactly two minutes, but it seemed like an hour. Then I saw the flash of headlights. The car came around

48

the bend. She was at the wheel, and he was beside her with his crutches under his elbow on the door side. When the car got to the tree it stopped. That was exactly according to the play. Next came the ticklish part. It was how to get him out of the car for a minute, with the bags in back and everything all set, so I could get in. If he had been all right on his two feet there would have been nothing to it, but getting a cripple out of a car once he gets set, and especially with a well person sitting right beside him, is like getting a hippopotamus out of a car.

She opened up just like I had coached her. 'I haven't got my pocketbook.'

'Didn't you take it?'

'I thought so. Look on the back seat.'

'No, nothing back there but my stuff.'

'I can't think what I've done with it.'

'Well come on, we'll be late. Here, here's a dollar. That'll be enough till you get back.'

'I must have left it on the sofa. In the living room.'

'Well all right, all right, you left it on the sofa in the living room. Now get going.'

She was coming to the part I had taken her over forty times. She was all for *asking* him to step out and get it. I finally beat it into her head that if she did that, she was just setting herself up to him to ask her why *she* didn't step out and get it, so he wouldn't have to unlimber the crutches. I showed her that her only chance was to talk dumb, not start the car, and wait him out, until he would get so sore, and so worried over the time, that he would make a martyr out of himself and get it himself. She kept at it, just like she was coached.

'But I want my pocketbook.'

'What for? Isn't a buck enough?'

'But it's got my lipstick in it.'

'Listen, can't you get it through your head we're trying to catch a train? This isn't an automobile trip, where we start when we get ready. It's a railroad train, and it goes at nine-forty-five, and when it goes it goes. Come on. Start up.'

'Well if you're going to talk that way.'

'What way?'

'All I said was that I wanted my—'

He ripped out a flock of cusswords, and at last I heard the crutches rattling against the side of the car. As soon as he was around the bend, hobbling back to the house, I dove in. I had to dive in the front door and climb over the seat into the back, so he wouldn't hear the back door close. That's a sound that always catches your ear, a car door closing. I crouched down there in the dark. He had his bag and his briefcase on the seat.

'Did I do it all right, Walter?'

'OK so far. How did you get rid of Lola?'

'I didn't have to. She was invited to something over at UCLA and I took her to the bus at seven.'

'OK. Back up, now, so he won't have so far to walk. Try and smooth him down.'

'All right.'

She backed up to the door and he got in again. She started off. Believe me it's an awful thing to kibbitz on a man and his wife, and hear what they really talk about. Soon as she got him a little smoothed down, he began to beef about Belle, the way she passed things at dinner. She panned Belle for the way she broke so many dishes. Then they got switched off to somebody named Hobey, and a woman named Ethel, that seemed to be Hobey's wife. He said he was through with Hobey and Hobey might as well know it. She said she used to like Ethel but the high-hat way she's been acting lately was too much. They figured it out whether they owed Hobey and Ethel a dinner or the other way around, so they found out they were one down, and decided that after they knocked that one off that was going to be the end of it. When they got that all settled, they decided he was to take a taxi wherever he went, up to Palo Alto, even if it did cost a little money. Because if he had to slog along on crutches everywhere he went, he wouldn't have a good time, and besides he might strain his leg. Phyllis talked just like he was going to Palo Alto, and she didn't have a thing on her mind. A woman is a funny animal.

Back where I was, I couldn't see where we were. I was even afraid to breathe, for fear he'd hear me. She was to drive so she didn't make any sudden stops, or get herself tangled in traffic, or do anything that would make him turn his head around to see what was back of us. He didn't. He had a cigar in his mouth, and lay back in the seat, smoking it. After a while she gave two sharp raps on the horn. That was our signal that we had come to a dark street we had picked out, about a half mile from the station.

I raised up, put my hand over his mouth, and pulled his head back. He grabbed my hand in both of his. The cigar was still in his fingers. I took it with my free hand and handed it to her. She took it. I took one of the crutches and hooked it under his chin. I won't tell you what I did then. But in two seconds he was curled down

on the seat with a broken neck, and not a mark on him
except a crease right over his nose, from the crosspiece of
the crutch.

6

We were right up with it, the moment of audacity that has to be the part of any successful murder. For the next twenty minutes we were in the jaws of death, not for what would happen now, but for how it would go together later. She started to throw the cigar out, but I stopped her. He had lit that cigar in the house, and I had to have it. She held it for me, and wiped the end of it as well as she could, while I went to work with the rope. I ran it across his shoulders, just below the neck, under his arms, and across his back. I tied it hard, and hooked the handle on, so it caught both sections of the rope, and drew them tight. A dead man is about the hardest thing to handle there is, but I figured with this harness we could do it, and do it quick.

'We're there, Walter. Shall I park now or drive around the block?'

'Park now. We're ready.'

She stopped. It was on a side street, about a block from the station. That stumped us for a while, where to park. If we went on the regular station parking lot, it was a 10 to 1 shot that a redcap would jerk the door open to get the bags, and we'd be sunk. But parking here, we would be all right. If we got a chance, we were to have an argument about it in front of somebody, with me complaining about how far she made me walk, to cover up on something that might look a little funny, later.

She got out and took the bag and briefcase. He was one of the kind who puts his toilet articles in a briefcase, for use on the train, and that was a break for me, later. I wound up all windows, took the crutches, and got out. She locked the car. We left him right where he was, curled down on the seat, with the harness on him.

She went ahead with the bag and briefcase, and I came along behind, with the bandaged leg half lifted up, walking on the crutches. That looked like a woman making it easy for a cripple. Really, it was a way to keep the redcap from getting a good look at me when he took the bags. Soon as we got around the corner, in sight of the station, here came one, running. He did just what we figured on. He took the bags from her, and never waited for me at all.

'The nine forty-five for San Francisco, Section 8, Car C.'

'Eight in Car C, yas'm. Meet you on the train.'

We went in the station. I made her drop back on me, so if anything came up I could mumble to her. I had the glasses on, and my hat pulled down, but not too much. I kept my eyes down, like I was watching where I put the crutches. I kept the cigar in my mouth, partly so it covered some of my face, partly so I could screw my face out of shape a little, like I was trying to keep the smoke out of my eyes.

The train was on a siding, out back of the station. I

made a quick count of the cars. 'Holy smoke, it's the third one.' It was the one that both conductors were standing in front of, and not only them, but the porter, and the redcap, waiting for his tip. Unless we did something quick, it would be four people that had a good look at me before I went in the car, and it might hang us. She ran on ahead. I saw her tip the redcap, and he went off, all bows. He didn't pass near me. He headed for the far end of the station, where the parking lot was. Then the porter saw me, and started for me. She took him by the arm. 'He doesn't like to be helped.'

The porter didn't get it. The Pullman conductor did. 'Hey!'

The porter stopped. Then he got it. They all turned their backs and started to talk. I stumped up the car steps. I got to the top. That was her cue. She was still down on the ground, with the conductors. 'Dear.'

I stopped and half turned. 'Come back to the observation platform. I'll say good-bye to you there, and then I won't have to worry about getting off the train. You still have a few minutes. Maybe we can talk.'

'Fine.'

I started back, through the car. She started back, on the ground, outside.

All three cars were full of people ready to go to bed, with most of the berths made up and bags all out in the aisle. The porters weren't there. They were at their boxes, outside. I kept my eyes down, clinched the cigar in my teeth, and kept my face screwed up. Nobody really saw me, and yet everybody saw me, because the minute they saw those crutches they began snatching bags out of the way and making room. I just nodded and mumbled 'thanks.'

When I saw her face I knew something was wrong. Outside on the observation platform, I saw what it was. A man was there, tucked back in a corner in the dark, having a smoke. I sat down on the opposite side. She reached her hand over. I took it. She kept looking at me for a cue. I kept making my lips say, 'Parking . . . parking . . . parking.' After a second or two she got it.

'Dear.'

'Yes?'

'You're not mad at me any more? For where I parked?'

'Forget it.'

'I thought I was headed for the station parking lot, honestly. But I get all mixed up in this part of town. I hadn't any idea I was going to make you walk so far.'

'I told you, forget it.'

'I'm terribly sorry.'

'Kiss me.'

I looked at my watch, held it up to her. It was still seven minutes before the train would leave. She needed a six-minute start for what she had to do. 'Listen, Phyllis, there's no use of you waiting around here. Why don't you blow?'

'Well – you don't mind?'

'Not a bit. No sense dragging it out.'

'Good-bye, then.'

'Good-bye.'

'Have a good time. Three cheers for Leland Stanford.'

'I'll do my best.'

'Kiss me again.'

'Good-bye.'

For what I had to do, I had to get rid of this guy, and get rid of him quick. I hadn't expected anybody out there. There seldom is when a train pulls out. I sat there, trying to think of something. I thought he might leave when he finished his cigarette, but he didn't. He threw it over the side and began to talk.

'Women are funny.'

'Funny and then some.'

'I couldn't help hearing that little conversation you had with your wife just now. About where she parked, I mean. Reminds me of an experience I had with my wife, coming home from San Diego.'

He told the experience he had with his wife. I looked him over. I couldn't see his face. I figured he couldn't see mine. He stopped talking. I had to say something.

'Yeah, women are funny all right. Specially when you get them behind the wheel of a car.'

'They're all of that.'

The train began to roll. It crawled through the outskirts of Los Angeles, and he kept on talking. Then an idea came to me. I remembered I was supposed to be a cripple, and began feeling through my pockets.

'You lose something?'

'My ticket. I can't find it.'

'Say, I wonder if I've got my ticket. Yeah, here it is.'

'You know what I bet she did? Put that ticket in my briefcase, right where I told her not to. She was to put it here in the pocket of this suit, and now—'

'Oh, it'll turn up.'

'Don't that beat all? Here I've got to go and hobble all through those cars, just because—'

'Don't be silly. Stay where you are.'

'No, I couldn't let you—'

'Be a pleasure old man. Stay right where you are and I'll get it for you. What's your space?'

'Would you? Section 8, Car C.'

'I'll be right back with it.'

We were picking up speed a little now. My mark was a dairy sign, about a quarter of a mile from the track. We came in sight of it and I lit the cigar. I put the crutches under one arm, threw my leg over the rail, and let myself down. One of the crutches hit the ties and spun me so I almost fell. I hung on. When we came square abreast of the sign I dropped off.

7

There's nothing so dark as a railroad track in the middle of the night. The train shot ahead, and I crouched there, waiting for the tingle to leave my feet. I had dropped off the left side of the train, into the footpath between the tracks, so there wouldn't be any chance I could be seen from the highway. It was about two hundred feet away. I stayed there, on my hands and knees, straining to see something on the other side of the tracks. There was a dirt road there, that gave entry to a couple of small factories, further on back. All around it were vacant lots, and it wasn't lit. She ought to be there by now. She had a seven-minute start, the train took six minutes to that point, and it was an eleven-minute drive from the station to this dirt road. I had checked it twenty times. I held still and stared, trying to spot the car. I couldn't see it.

I don't know how long I crouched there. It came to me that maybe she had bumped somebody's fender, or been stopped by a cop, or something. I seemed to turn to water. Then I heard something. I heard a panting. Then with it I heard footsteps. They would go fast for a second or two, and then stop. It was like being in a nightmare, with something queer coming after me, and I didn't know what it was, but it was horrible. Then I saw it. It was her. That man must have weighed 200 pounds, but she had him on her back, holding him by the handle, and staggering along with him, over the tracks. His head was hanging down beside her head. They looked like something in a horror picture.

I ran over and grabbed his legs, to take some of the weight off her. We ran him a few steps. She started to throw him down. 'Not that track! The other one!'

We got him over to the track the train went out on, and dropped him. I cut the harness off and slipped it in my pocket. I put the lighted cigar within a foot or two of him. I threw one crutch over him and the other beside the track.

'Where's the car?'

'There. Couldn't you see it?'

I looked, and there it was, right where it was supposed to be, on the dirt road.

'We're done. Let's go.'

We ran over and climbed in and she started the motor, threw in the gear. 'Oh my – his hat!'

I took the hat and sailed it out the window, on the tracks. 'It's OK, a hat can roll, – *get going!*'

She started up. We passed the factories. We came to a street.

On Sunset she went through a light. 'Watch that stuff, can't you, Phyllis? If you're stopped now, with me in the car, we're sunk.'

'Can I drive with that thing going on?'

She meant the car radio. I had it turned on. It was to be part of my alibi, for the time I was out of the house, that I knocked off work for a while and listened to the radio. I had to know what was coming in that night. I had to know more than I could find out by reading the programs in the papers. 'I've got to have it, you know that—'

'Let me alone, let me drive!'

She hit a zone, and must have been doing seventy. I clenched my teeth, and kept quiet. When we came to a vacant lot I threw out the rope. About a mile further on I threw out the handle. Going by a curb drain I shot the glasses into it. Then I happened to look down and saw her shoes. They were scarred from the track ballast.

'What did you carry him for? Why didn't you let me—'

'Where were you? *Where were you?*'

'I was there. I was waiting—'

'Did I know that? Could I just sit there, with *that* in the car?'

'I was trying to see where you were. I couldn't see—'

'Let me alone, *let me drive!*'

'Your shoes—'

I choked it back. In a second or two, she started up again. She raved like a lunatic. She raved and she kept on raving, about him, about me, about anything that came in her head. Every now and then I'd snap. There we were, after what we had done, snarling at each other like a couple of animals, and neither one of us could stop. It was like somebody had shot us full of some kind of dope. 'Phyllis, cut this out. We've got to talk, and it may be our last chance.'

'Talk then! Who's stopping you?'

'First then: You don't know anything about this insurance policy. You—'

'How many times do you have to say that?'

'I'm only telling you—'

'You've already told me till I'm sick of hearing you.'

'Next, the inquest. You bring—'

'I bring a minister, I know that, I bring a minister to take charge of the body, how many times have I got to listen to that – *are you going to let me drive?*'

'OK, then. Drive.'

'Is Belle home?'

'How do I know? No!'

'And Lola's out?'

'Didn't I tell you?'

'Then you'll have to stop at the drugstore. To get a pint of ice cream or something. To have witnesses you drove straight home from the station. You got to say something to fix the time and the date. You—'

'Get out! Get out! I'll go insane!'

'I can't get out. I've got to get to my car! Do you know what that means, if I take time to walk? I can't complete my alibi! I—'

'I said get out!'

'Drive on, or I'll sock you.'

When she got to my car she stopped and I got out. We didn't kiss. We didn't even say good-bye. I got out of her car, got in mine, started, and drove home.

When I got home I looked at the clock. It was 10:25. I opened the bell box of the telephone. The card was still there. I closed the box and dropped the card in my pocket. I went in the kitchen and looked at the doorbell. That card was still there. I dropped it in my pocket. I went upstairs, ripped off my clothes, and got into pajamas and slippers. I cut the bandage of my foot. I went down, shoved the bandage and cards into the fireplace, with a newspaper, and lit it. I watched it burn. Then I went to the telephone and started to dial. I still had one call-back to get, to round out the late part of my alibi. I felt something like a drawstring pull in my throat, and a sob popped out of me. I clapped the phone down. It was getting me. I knew I had to get myself under some kind of control. I swallowed a couple of times. I wanted to make sure of my voice, that it would sound OK. A dumb idea came to me that maybe if I would sing something, that would make me snap out of it. I started to sing the 'Isle of Capri.' I sang about two notes, and it swallowed into a kind of a wail.

I went in the dining room and took a drink. I took another drink. I started mumbling to myself, trying to get so I could talk. I had to have something to mumble. I thought of the Lord's Prayer. I mumbled that, a couple of times. I tried to mumble it another time, and couldn't remember how it went.

When I thought I could talk, I dialed again. I was 10:48. I dialed Ike Schwartz, that's another salesman with General.

'Ike, do me a favor, will you? I'm trying to figure out a proposition on a public liability bond for a wine company to have it ready for them tomorrow morning, and I'm going nuts. I came off without my rate book.

Joe Pete can't find it, and I'm wondering if you'll look up what I want in yours. You got it with you?'

'Sure, I'll be glad to.'

I gave him the dope. He said give him fifteen minutes and he'd call back.

I walked around, digging my fingernails into my hands, trying to hold on to myself. The drawstring began to jerk on my throat again. I began mumbling again, saying over and over what I had just said to Ike. The phone rang. I answered. He had it figured for me, he said, and began to give it to me. He gave it to me three different ways, so I'd have it all. It took him twenty minutes. I took it down, what he said. I could feel the sweat squeezing out on my forehead and running down off my nose. After a while he was done.

'OK, Ike, that's just what I wanted to know. That's just how I wanted it. Thanks a thousand times.'

Soon as he hung up everything cracked. I dived for the bathroom. I was sicker than I had ever been in my life. After that passed I fell into bed. It was a long time before I could turn out the light. Then I lay there staring into the dark. Every now and then I would have a chill or something and start to tremble. Then that passed and I lay there, like a dope. Then I started to think. I tried not to, but it would creep up on me. I knew then what I had done. I had killed a man. I had killed a man to get a woman. I had put myself in her power, so there was one person in the world that could point a finger at me, and I would have to die. I had done all that for her, and I never wanted to see her again as long as I lived.

That's all it takes, one drop of fear, to curdle love into hate.

gulped down some orange juice and coffee, and then went up in the bedroom with the paper. I was afraid to open it in front of the Filipino. Sure enough, there it was, on Page 1:

OIL MAN, ON WAY TO JUNE RALLY, DIES IN TRAIN FALL

H. S. Nirdlinger, Petroleum Pioneer, Killed In Plunge from Express En Route to Reunion At Leland Stanford. With injuries about the head and neck, the body of H. S. Nirdlinger, Los Angeles representative of the Western Pipe & Supply Company and for a number of years prominently identified with the oil industry here, was found on the railroad tracks about two miles north of this city shortly before midnight last night. Mr Nirdlinger had departed on a northbound train earlier in the evening to attend his class reunion at Leland Stanford University, and it is believed he fell from the train. Police point out he had fractured his leg some weeks ago, and believe his unfamiliarity with crutches may have caused him to lose his balance on the observation platform, where he was last seen alive.

Mr Nirdlinger was 44 years old. Born in Fresno, he attended Leland Stanford, and on graduation, entered the oil business, becoming one of the pioneers in the opening of the field at Long Beach. Later he was active at Signal Hill. For the last three years he had been in charge of the local office of the Western Pipe & Supply Company.

Surviving are a widow, formerly Miss Phyllis Belden of Mannerheim, and a daughter, Miss Lola Nirdlinger. Mrs Nirdlinger, before her marriage, was head nurse of the Verdugo Health Institute here.

Twenty minutes to nine, Nettie called. She said Mr Norton wanted to see me, as soon as I could possibly get down. That meant they already had it, and I wouldn't have to put on any act, going in there with my paper and saying this is the guy I sold an accident policy to last winter. I said I knew what it was, and I was right on my way.

I got through the day somehow. I think I told you about Norton and Keyes. Norton is president of the company. He's a short, stocky man about 35, that got the job when his father died and he's so busy trying to act like his father he doesn't seem to have time for much else. Keyes is head of the Claim Department, a holdover from the old regime, and the way he tells it young Norton never does anything right. He's big and fat and peevish, and on top of that he's a theorist, and it makes your head ache to be around him, but he's the best claim man on the Coast, and he was the one I was afraid of.

First I had to face Norton, and tell him what I knew, or anyway what I was supposed to know. I told him how I propositioned Nirdlinger about the accident policy, and how his wife and daughter opposed it, and how I dropped it that night but went over to his office a couple of days later to give him another whirl. That would check with what the secretary saw. I told him how I sold him, then, but only after I promised not to say anything to the wife and daughter about it. I told how I took his application, then when the policy came through, delivered it, and got his check. Then we went down in Keyes's office and we went all over it again. It took all morning, you understand. All while we were talking phone calls and telegrams kept coming in, from San Francisco, where Keyes had our investigators inter-viewing people that were on the train, from the police, from the secrtary, from Lola, after they got her on the phone to find out what she knew. They tried to get Phyllis, but she had strict instruction from me not to come to the phone, so she didn't. They got hold of the coroner, and arranged for an autopsy. There's generally a hook-up between insurance companies and coroners, so they can get an autopsy if they want it. They could demand it, under a clause in their policy, but that would mean going to court for an order, and would tip it that the deceased was insured, and that's bad all the way round. They get it on the quiet, and in this case they had to have it. Because if Nirdlinger died of apoplexy, or heart failure, and fell off the train, then it wouldn't any longer be accident, but death from natural causes, and they wouldn't be liable. About the middle of the afternoon they got the medical report. Death was from a broken neck. When they heard that they got the inquest postponed two days.

By four o'clock, the memos and telegrams were piled on Keyes's desk so he had to put a weight on top of them to keep them from falling over, and he was mopping his brow and so peevish nobody could talk to him. But Norton was getting more cheerful by the minute. He took a San Francisco call from somebody named Jackson, and I could tell from what he said that it was this guy I had got rid of on the observation platform before I dropped off. When he hung up he put one more memo on top of the others and turned to Keyes. 'Clear case of suicide.'

If it was suicide, you see, the company wouldn't be liable either. This policy only covered accident.

'Yeah?'

'All right, watch me while I check it over. First, he took out this policy. He took it out in secret. He didn't tell his wife, he didn't tell his daughter, he didn't tell his secretary, he didn't tell anybody. If Huff here, had been on the job, he might have known—'

'Known what?'

'No need to get sore, Huff. But you've got to admit it looked funny.'

'It didn't look funny at all. It happens every day. Now if *they* had tried to insure *him*, without *him* knowing, *that* would have looked funny.'

'That's right. Leave Huff out of it.'

'All I'm saying, Keyes, is that—'

'Huff's record shows that if there had been anything funny, he'd have noted it and we'd have known it. You better find out something about your own agents.'

'All right, skip it. He takes out this policy in absolute secrecy. Why? Because he knew that if his family knew what he had done, they would know what he was up to. They knew what was on his mind, we can depend on that, and when we go into his books and his history, we'll find out what the trouble was. All right, next point, he fractured his leg, but he didn't put a claim in. Why? That looks funny, don't it, that a man had an accident policy, and didn't put a claim in for a broken leg? *Because he knew he was going to do this, and he was afraid if he put a claim in the family would find out about this policy and block him off.'*

'How?'

'If they called us up, we'd cancel on him, wouldn't we? You bet we would. We'd return his unused premium so fast you couldn't see our dust, and he knew it. Oh no, he wasn't taking a chance on our doctor going out there to look at his leg and tipping things off. That's a big point.'

'Go on.'

'All right, he figures an excuse to take a train. He takes his wife with him to the station, he gets on the train, he gets rid of her. She goes. He's ready to do it. But he runs into trouble. There's a guy out there, on the observation platform, and for this he don't want any company. You bet he doesn't. So what does he do? He gets rid of him, by putting up some kind of a story about not having his ticket, and leaving it in his briefcase, and as soon as this guy goes, he takes his dive. That was the guy I just talked to, a man by the name of Jackson that went up to Frisco on a business trip and is coming back tomorrow. He says there's no question about it, he had the feeling even when he offered to get Nirdlinger's briefcase for him that he was trying to get rid of him, but he didn't quite have the heart to say no to a cripple. In my mind, that clinches it. It's a clear case of suicide. You can't take any other view of it.'

'So what?'

'Our next step is the inquest. We can't appear there, of course, because if a jury finds out a dead man is insured they'll murder us. We can send an investigator or two, perhaps, to sit in there, but nothing more than that. But Jackson says he'll be glad to appear and tell what he knows, and there's a chance, just a chance, but still a chance, that we may get a suicide verdict anyway. If we do, we're in. If we don't, then we've got to consider what we do. However, one thing at a time. The inquest first, and you can't tell what the police may find out; we may win right in the first round.'

Keyes mopped his head some more. He was so fat he really suffered in the heat. He lit a cigarette. He dropped down and looked away from Norton like it was some schoolboy and he didn't want to show his disgust. Then he spoke. 'It was not suicide.'

'What are you talking about? It's a clear case.'

'It was not suicide.'

He opened his bookcase and began throwing thick books on the table. 'Mr Norton, here's what the actuaries have to say about suicide. You study them, you might find out something about the insurance business.'

'I was raised in the insurance business, Keyes.'

'You were raised in private schools, Groton, and Harvard. While you were learning how to pull bow oars there, I was studying these tables. Take a look at them. Here's suicide by race, by color, by occupation, by sex, by locality, by seasons of the year, by time of day when committed. Here's suicide by method of accomplishment. Here's method of accomplishment subdivided by poisons, by firearms, by gas, by drowning, by leaps.

Here's suicide by poisons subdivided by sex, by race, by age, by time of day. Here's suicide by poisons subdivided by cyanide, by mercury, by strychnine, by thirty-eight other poisons, sixteen of them no longer procurable at prescription pharmacies. And here – here, Mr Norton – are leaps subdivided by leaps from high places, under wheels of moving trains, under wheels of trucks, under the feet of horses, from steamboats. But *there's not one case here out of all these millions of cases of a leap from the rear end of a moving train.* That's just one way they don't do it.'

'They could.'

'Could they? That train, at the point where the body was found, moves at a maximum of fifteen miles an hour. Could any man jump off it there with any real expectation of killing himself?'

'He might dive off. This man had a broken neck.'

'Don't trifle with me. He wasn't an acrobat.'

'Then what are you trying to tell me? That it was on the up-and-up?'

'Listen, Mr Norton. When a man takes out an insurance policy, an insurance policy that's worth $50,000 if he's killed in a railroad accident, and then three months later he is killed in a railroad accident, it's not on the up-and-up. It can't be. If the train got wrecked it might be, but even then it would be a mighty suspicious coincidence. A *mighty* suspicious coincidence. No, it's not on the up-and-up. But it's not suicide.'

'Then what do you mean?'

'You know what I mean.'

'... Murder?'

'I mean murder.'

'Well wait a minute, Keyes, wait a minute. Wait till I catch up with you. What have you got to go on?'

'Nothing.'

'You must have *something*.'

'I said nothing. Whoever did this did a perfect job. There's nothing to go on. Just the same, it's murder.'

'Do you suspect anybody?'

'The beneficiary of such a policy, so far as I am concerned, is automatically under suspicion.'

'You mean the wife?'

'I mean the wife.'

'She wasn't even on the train.'

'Then somebody else was.'

'Have you any idea who?'

'None at all.'

'And this is all you have to go on?'

'I told you, I have nothing to go on. Nothing but those tables and my own hunch, instinct, and experience. It's a slick job, but it's no accident, and it's no suicide.'

'Then what are we going to do?'

'I don't know. Give me a minute to think.'

He took a half hour to think. Norton and I, we sat there and smoked. After a while, Keyes bgan to bump the desk with the palm of his hand. He knew what he meant, you could see that.

'Mr Norton.'

'Yes, Keyes.'

'There's only one thing for you to do. It's against practice, and in some other case I'd oppose it. But not in this. There's a couple of things about this that make me think that practice is one of the things they're going to count on, and take advantage of. Practice in a case like this is to wait, and make them come to you, isn't it? I advise against that. I advise jumping in there at once, tonight if possible, and if not tonight, then certainly on the day of that inquest, and filing a complaint against that woman. I advise filing an information of suspected murder against her, and smashing at her as hard and as quick as we can. I advise that we demand her arrest, and her detention too, for the full forty-eight hours incommunicado that the law allows in a case of this kind. I advise sweating her with everything the police have got. I particularly advise separating her from this accomplice, whoever he is, or she is, so we get the full value of surprise, and prevent their conferring in future plans. Do that, and mark my words you're going to find out things that'll amaze you.'

'But – *on what?*'

'On nothing.'

'But Keyes, we can't do a thing like that. Suppose we don't find out anything. Suppose we sweat her and get nothing. Suppose it *is* on the up-and-up. Look where that puts us. Holy smoke, she could murder us in a civil suit, and a jury would give her every nickel she asks for. I'm not sure they couldn't get us for *criminal* libel. And then look at the other side of it. We've got an advertising budget of $100,000 a year. We describe ourselves as the friend of the widow and orphan. We spend all that for goodwill, and then what? We lay ourselves open to the charge that we'd accuse a woman of *murder* even, rather than pay a just claim.'

'It's not a just claim.'

'It will be, unless we prove different.'

'All right. What you say is true. I told you it's against practice. But let me tell you this, Mr Norton, and tell you right now: Whoever pulled this was no punk. He, or she, or maybe the both of them, or the three of them or however many it took – knew what they were doing. They're not going to be caught just by your sitting around hoping for clues. They thought of clues. There aren't any. The only way you're going to catch them is to move against *them*. I don't care if it's a battle or a murder case, or whatever it is, surprise is a weapon that *can* work. I don't say it will work. But I say it can work. And I say nothing else is going to work.'

'But Keyes, we can't do things like that.'

'Why not?'

'Keyes, we've been over that a million times, every insurance company has been over it a million times. We have our practice, and you can't beat it. These things are a matter for the police. We can help the police, if we've got something to help with. If we discover information, we can turn it over to them. If we have our suspicions, we can communicate them to them. We can take any lawful, legitimate step – but as for this—'

He stopped. Keyes waited, and he didn't finish.

'What's unlawful about this, Mr Norton?'

'Nothing. It's lawful enough – but it's wrong. It puts us out in the open. It leaves us with *no* defenses – in case we miss on it. I never heard of a thing like that. It's – tactically wrong, that's what I'm trying to say.'

'But strategically right.'

'We've got our strategy. We've got our ancient strategy, and you can't beat it. Listen, it *can* be suicide. We can affirm our belief that it's suicide, at the proper time, and we're safe. The burden of proof is on her. That's what I'm trying to say. Believe me, on a keg of dynamite like this, I don't want to get myself in the position where the burden of proof is on us.'

'You're not going to move against her?'

'Not yet, Keyes, not yet. Maybe later, I don't know. But so long as we can do the conservative, safe thing, I don't get mixed up with the other kind.'

'Your father—'

'Would have done the same thing. I'm thinking of him.'

'He would not. Old Man Norton could take a chance.'

'Well I'm not my father!'

'It's your responsibility.'

I didn't go to the inquest, Norton didn't, and Keyes didn't. No insurance company can afford to let a jury know, whether it's a coroner's jury or any other kind of jury, that a dead man is insured. It just gets murdered if that comes out. Two investigators were sent over, guys that look like everybody else and sit with the newspaper men. We got what happened from them. They all identified the body and told their story, Phyllis, the two conductors, the red-cap, the porter, a couple of passengers, the police, and especially this guy Jackson, that pounded it in that I tried to get rid of him. The jury brought in a verdict 'that the said Herbert S. Nirdlinger came to his death by a broken neck received in a fall from a railroad train at or about ten o'clock on the night of June 3 in a manner unknown to this jury.' It took Norton by surprise. He really hoped for a suicide verdict. It didn't me. The most important person at that inquest never said a word, and I had beat it into Phyllis's head long before that he had to be there, because I had figured on this suicide stuff, and we had to be ready for it. That was the minister that she asked to come with her, to confer with the undertaker on arrangements for the funeral. Once a coroner's jury sees that it's a question of burial in consecrated ground, the guy could take poison, cut his throat, and jump off the end of a dock, and they would still give a verdict, 'in a manner unknown to this jury.'

After the investigators told their story, we sat around again, Norton, Keyes, and myself, in Norton's office this time. It was about five o'clock in the afternoon. Keyes was sore. Norton was disappointed, but still trying to make it look like he had done the right thing. 'Well, Keyes, we're no worse off.'

'You're no better off.'

'Anyway, we haven't done anything foolish.'

'What now?'

'Now? I follow practice. I wait her out. I deny liability, on the ground that accident is not proved, and I make her sue. When she sues, then we'll see what we see.'

'You're sunk.'

'I know I'm sunk, but that's what I'm going to do.'

'What do you mean you know you're sunk?'

'Well, I've been talking to the police about this. I told them we suspect murder. They said they did too, at first, but they've given up that idea. They've gone into it. They've got their books too, Keyes. They know how people commit murder, and how they don't. They say they never heard of a case where murder was committed, or even attempted, by pushing a man off the rear end of a slow-moving train. They say the same thing about it you say. How could a murderer, assuming there was one, be sure the man would die? Suppose he only got hurt? Then where would they be? No, they assure me it's on the up-and-up. It's just one of those freak things, that's all.'

'Did they cover everybody that was on that train? Did they find out whether there was a single one of them that was acquainted with this wife? Holy smoke, Mr Norton, don't tell me they gave up without going into that part. I *tell you, there was somebody else on that train!*'

'They did better than that. They covered the observation car steward. He took a seat right by the door, to mark up his slips for the beginning of the trip, and he's certain nobody was out there with Nirdlinger, because if anybody had passed him he would have had to move. He remembers Jackson going out there, about ten minutes before the train pulled out. He remembers the cripple going by. He remembers Jackson coming back. He remembers Jackson going out there again with the briefcase, and Jackson coming back, the second time. Jackson didn't report the disappearance right away. He just figured Nirdlinger went in a washroom or something, and as a matter of fact, it wasn't till midnight, when he wanted to go to bed and he still had the briefcase that he supposed had Nirdlinger's ticket in it, that he said anything to the conductor about it. Five minutes after that, at Santa Barbara, was where the Los Angeles yardmaster caught the conductor with a wire and he impounded Nirdlinger's baggage and began taking names. There was nobody out there. This guy fell off, that's all. We're sunk. It's on the up-and-up.'

'If it's on the up-and-up, why don't you pay her?'

'Well wait a minute. That's what I think. That's what the police think. But there's still considerable evidence of suicide—'

'Not a scrap.'

'Enough, Keyes, that I owe it to my stockholders to throw the thing into court, and let a jury decide. I may be wrong. The police may be wrong. Before that suit comes to trial, we may be able to turn up plenty. That's all I'm going to do. Let a jury decide, and if it decides we're liable, then I pay her, and do it cheerfully. But I can't just make her a present of the money.'

'That's what you'll be doing, if you allege suicide.'

'We'll see.'

'Yeah, we'll see.'

I walked back with Keyes to his office. He snapped on the lights. 'He'll see. I've handled too many cases, Huff. When you've handled a million of them, you know, and you don't even know how you know. This is murder . . . So they covered the porter, did they. Nobody went out there. How do they know somebody didn't swing aboard from the outside? How do they know—'

He stopped, looked at me, and then he began to curse and rave like a maniac. 'Didn't I tell him? Didn't I tell him? Didn't I tell him too drive at her right from the start? Didn't I tell him to have her put under arrest, without waiting for this inquest? Didn't I tell him—'

'What do you mean, Keyes?' My heart was pounding, plenty.

'He was never on the train!'

He was yelling now, and pounding the desk. 'He was never on the train at all! Somebody took his crutches and went on the train for him! Of course that guy had to get rid of Jackson! He couldn't be seen alive beyond the point where that body was to be put! And now we've got all those sworn indentifications against us—'

'Those what?' I knew what he meant. Those identifications at the inquest were something I had figured on from the start, and that was why I took such care that nobody on that train got a good look at me. I figured the crutches, the foot, the glasses, the cigar, and imagination would be enough.

'At the inquest! How well did any of those witnesses see this man? Just a few seconds, in the dark, three or four days ago. Then the coroner lifts a sheet on a dead man, the widow says yes, that's him, and of course they all say the same thing. And now look at us! If Norton had thrown the gaff into her, all those identifications and everything else about it could have been challenged, the police would have waked up, and we might be somewhere. But now—! So he's going to let her sue! And just let him try, now, to break down those identifications. It'll be impossible. Any lawyer can crucify those witnesses if they change their story now. So that's being conservative! That's playing it safe! That's doing what the old man would have done! Why, Huff, Old Man Norton would have had a confession out of that woman by now. He'd have had a plea of guilty out of her, and already on her way to do a life stretch in Folsom. And now look at us. Just look at us. The very crux of the thing is over already, and we've lost it. We've lost it . . . Let me tell you something. If that guy keeps on trying to run this company, the company's sunk. You can't take many body blows like this and last. Holy smoke. Fifty thousand bucks, and all from dumbness. Just sheer, willful stupidity!'

The lights began to look funny in front of my eyes. He started up again, checking over how Nirdlinger got knocked off. He said this guy, whoever he was, had left his car at Burbank, and dropped off the train there. He said she met him there, and they drove down in separate cars, with the corpse in one of them, to the place where they put the body on the track. He figured it up that she would have time to get to Burbank, and then get back in time to buy a pint of ice cram at the drugstore at 10:20, when she showed up there. He even had that. He was all wrong on how it was done, but he was so near right it made my lips turn numb just to listen to him.

'Well, Keyes, what are you going to do?'

'. . . All right, he wants to wait her out, make her sue – that suits me. He's going to cover the dead man, find out what he can about why he maybe committed suicide. That suits me. I'm going to cover *her*. Every move she makes, everything she does, I'm going to know about it. Sooner or later, Huff, that guy's got to show. They'll have to see each other. And as soon as I know who he is, then watch me. Sure, let her sue. And when she goes on the witness stand, believe me, Huff, Norton's going to eat it. He's going to eat every word he's said, and the police may do some eating too. Oh no. I'm not through yet.'

*

He had me, and I knew it. If she sued, and lost her head on the witness stand, God knows what might happpen. If she didn't sue, that would be still worse. Her not trying to collect on that policy, that would look so bad it might even pull the police in. I didn't dare call her up, because for all I knew even now her wires might be tapped. I did that night what I had done the other two nights, while I was waiting on the inquest. I got stinko, or tried to. I knocked off a quart of cognac, but it didn't have any effect. My legs felt funny, and my ears rang, but my eyes kept staring at the dark, and my mind kept pounding on it, what I was going to do. I didn't know. I couldn't sleep, I couldn't eat, I couldn't even get drunk.

It was the next night before Phyllis called. It was a little while after dinner, and the Filipino had just gone. I was even afraid to answer, but I knew I had to. 'Walter?'

'Yes. First, where are you? Home?'

'I'm in a drugstore.'

'Oh. OK, then, go on.'

'Lola's acting so funny I don't even want to use my own phone any more. I drove down to the boulevard.'

'What's the matter with Lola?'

'Oh, just hysteria, I guess. It's been too much for her.'

'Nothing else?'

'I don't think so.'

'All right, shoot, and shoot quick. What's happened?'

'An awful lot. I've been afraid to call. I had to stay home until the funeral, and—'

'The funeral was today?'

'Yes. After the inquest.'

'Go on.'

'The next thing, tomorrow they open my husband's safe deposit box. The state has something to do with that. On account of the inheritance tax.'

'That's right. The policy's in there?'

'Yes. I put it in there about a week ago.'

'All right then, this is what you do. It'll be at your lawyer's office, is that it?'

'Yes.'

'Then you go there. The state tax man will be there, under the law he has to be present. They'll find the policy, and you hand it to your lawyer. Instruct him to put your claim in. Everything waits until you do that.'

'Put the claim in.'

'That's right. Now wait a minute, Phyllis. Here's something you mustn't tell that lawyer – yet. They're not going to pay that claim.'

'What!'

'They're not going to pay it.'

'Don't they have to pay it?'

'They think it's – suicide – and they're going to make you sue, and put it in the hands of a jury, before they pay. Don't tell your lawyer that now, he'll find it out for himself later. He'll want to sue, and you let him. We'll have to pay him, but it's our only chance. Now Phyllis, one other thing.'

'Yes.'

'I can't see you.'

'But I want to see you.'

'We don't dare see each other. Suicide is what they hope for, but they're mighty suspicious all the way around. If you and I began seeing each other, they might tumble to the truth so fast it would make your blood run cold. They'll be on your trail, for what they can find out, and you simply must not communicate with me at all, unless it's imperative, and even then you must call me at home, and from a drugstore, never the same drugstore twice in succession. Do you get me?'

'My you sound scared.'

'I am scared. Plenty. They know more than you'd think.'

'Then it's really serious?'

'Maybe not, but we've got to be careful.'

'Then maybe I'd better not sue.'

'You've *got* to sue. If you don't sue, then we *are* sunk.'

'Oh. Oh. Yes, I can see that.'

'You sue. But be careful what you tell that lawyer.'

'All right. Do you still love me?'

'You know I do.'

'Do you think of me? All the time?'

'All the time.'

'Is there anything else?'

'Not that I know of. Is that all with you?'

'I think so.'

'You better hang up. Somebody might come in on me.'

'You sound as though you want to get rid of me.'

'Just common sense.'

'All right. How long is this all going to take?'

'I don't know. Maybe quite some time.'

'I'm dying to see you.'

'Me too. But we've got to be careful.'

'Well then – good-bye.'

'Good-bye.'

*

I hung up. I loved her like a rabbit loves a rattlesnake. That night I did something I hadn't done in years. I prayed.

9

It was about a week after that Nettie came into my private office quick and shut the door. 'That Miss Nirdlinger to see you again Mr Huff.'

'Hold her a minute. I've got to make a call.'

She went out. I made a call. I had to do something to get myself in hand. I called home, and asked the Filipino if there had been any calls. He said no. Then I buzzed Nettie to send her in.

She looked different from the last time I had seen her. Then, she looked like a kid. Now, she looked like a woman. Part of that may have been that she was in black, but anybody could see she had been through plenty. I felt like a heel, and yet it did something to me that this girl liked me. I shook hands with her, and sat her down, and asked her how her stepmother was, and she said she was all right, considering everything, and I said it was a terrible thing, and that it shocked me to hear of it. 'And Mr Sachetti?'

'I'd rather not talk about Mr Sachetti.'

'I thought you were friends.'

'I'd rather not talk about him.'

'I'm sorry.'

She got up, looked out the window, then sat down again. 'Mr Huff, you did something for me once, or anyhow I felt it was for me—'

'It was.'

'And since then I've always thought of you as a friend. That's why I've come to you. I want to talk to you – as a friend.'

'Certainly.'

'But only as a friend, Mr Huff. Not as somebody – in the insurance business. Until I feel I know my own mind, it has to be in the strictest confidence. Is that understood, Mr Huff?'

'It is.'

'I'm forgetting something. I was to call you Walter.'

'And I was to call you Lola.'

'It's funny how easy I feel with you.'

'Go ahead.'

'It's about my father.'

'Yes?'

'My father's death. I can't help feeling there was something back of it.'

'I don't quite understand you, Lola. How do you mean, back of it?'

'I don't know what I mean.'

'You were at the inquest?'

'Yes.'

'One or two witnesses there, and several people later, to us, intimated that your father might have – killed himself. Is that what you mean?'

'No, Walter, it isn't.'

'Then what?'

'I can't say. I can't make myself say it. And it's so

awful. Because this isn't the first time I've had such thoughts. This isn't the first time I've been through this agony of suspicion that there might be something more than – what everybody else thinks.'

'I still don't follow you.'

'My mother.'

'Yes.'

'When she died. That's how I felt.'

I waited. She swallowed two or three times, looked like she had decided not to say anything at all, then changed her mind again and started to talk.

'Walter, my mother had lung trouble. It was on account of that that we kept a little shack up at Lake Arrowhead. One weekend, in the middle of winter, my mother went up to that shack with her dearest friend. It was right in the middle of the winter sports, when everything was lively up there, and then she wired my father that she and this other woman had decided to stay on for a week. He didn't think anything of it, wired her a little money, and told her to stay as long as she wanted; he thought it would do her good. Wednesday of that week my mother caught pneumonia. Friday her condition became critical. Her friend walked twelve miles through snowdrifts, through the woods, to get a doctor – the shack isn't near the hotels. It's on the other side of the lake, a long way around. She got into the main hotel there so exhausted she had to be sent to a hospital. The doctor started out, and when he got there my mother was dying. She lived a half hour.'

'Yes?'

'Do you know who that best friend was?'

I knew. I knew by the same old prickle that was going up my back and into my hair. 'No.'

'Phyllis.'

'. . . Well?'

'What were those two women doing in that shack, all that time, in the dead of the winter? Why didn't they go to the hotel, like everybody else? Why didn't my mother telephone, instead of wiring?'

'You mean it wasn't she that wired?'

'I don't know what I mean, except that it looked mighty funny. Why did Phyllis tramp all that distance to get a doctor? Why didn't she stop some place, and telephone? Or why didn't she put on her skates, and go across the lake, which she could have done in a half hour? She's a fine skater. Why did she take that three-hour trip? *Why didn't she go for a doctor sooner?*'

'But wait a minute. What did your mother say to the doctor when he—'

'Nothing. She was in high delirium, and besides he had her in oxygen five minutes after he got there.'

'But wait a minute, Lola. After all, a doctor is a doctor, and if she *had* pneumonia—'

'A doctor is a doctor, but you don't know Phyllis. There's some things I could tell. In the first place, she's a nurse. She's one of the best nurses in the city of Los Angeles – that's how she met my mother, when my mother was having such a terrible fight to live. She's a nurse, and she specialized in pulmonary diseases. She would know the time of crisis, almost to a minute, as well as any doctor would. And she would know how to bring on pneumonia, too.'

'What do you mean by that?'

'You think Phyllis wouldn't be capable of putting my mother out in the night, in that cold, and keeping her locked out until she was half frozen to death – you think Phyllis wouldn't do that? You think she's just the dear, sweet, gentle thing that she looks like? That's what my father thought. He thought it was wonderful, the way she trudged all that distance to save a life, and less than a year after that he married her. But I don't think so. You see – I know her. That's what I thought, the minute I heard it. And now – this.'

'What do you want me to do?'

'Nothing – yet. Except listen to me.'

'It's pretty serious, what you're saying. Or at any rate intimating. I suppose I know what you mean.'

'That's what I mean. That's exactly what I mean.'

'However, as I understand it, your mother wasn't *with* your father at the time.'

'She wasn't with my mother either. At the time. But she had been.'

'Will you let me think this over?'

'Please do.'

'You're a little wrought up today.'

'And I haven't told you all.'

'What else?'

'. . . I can't tell you. That, I can't make myself believe. And yet – never mind. Forgive me, Walter, for coming in here like this. But I'm so unhappy.'

'Have you said anything to anybody about this?'

'No, nothing.'

'I mean – about your mother? Before this last?'

'Not a word, ever, to anybody.'

'I wouldn't if I were you. And especially not to – your stepmother.'

'I'm not even living home now.'

'No?'

'I've take a little apartment. Down in Hollywood. I have a little income. From my mother's estate. Just a little. I moved out. I couldn't live with Phyllis any more.'

'Oh.'

'Can I come in again?'

'I'll let you know when to come. Give me your number.'

I spent half the afternoon trying to make up my mind whether to tell Keyes. I knew I ought to tell him, for my own protection. It was nothing that would be worth a nickel as evidence in court, and for that matter it was nothing that any court would admit as evidence, because that's one break they give people, that they have to be tried for one thing at a time, and not for something somebody thinks they did two or three years before this happened. But it was something that would look mighty bad, if Keyes found out I knew it, and hadn't told him. I couldn't make myself do it. And I didn't have any better reason than that this girl had asked me not to tell anybody, and I had promised.

About four o'clock Keyes came in my office and shut the door.

'Well, Huff, he's showed.'

'Who?'

'The guy in the Nirdlinger case.'

'*What?*'

'He's a steady caller now. Five nights in one week.'

'. . . Who is he?'

'Never mind. But he's the one. Now watch me.'

That night I came back in the office to work. As soon as Joe Pete made his eight o'clock round on my floor I went to Keyes's office. I tried his desk. It was locked. I tried his steel filing cabinets. They were locked. I tried all my keys. They didn't work. I was about to give it up when I noticed the dictation machine. He uses one of them. I took the cover off it. A record was still on. It was about three quarters filled. I made sure Joe Pete was downstairs, then came back, slipped the ear pieces on and started the record. First a lot of dumb stuff came out, letters to claimants, instructions to investigators on an arson case, notification of a clerk that he was fired. Then, all of a sudden, came this:

Memo. to Mr Norton
Re. Agent Walter Huff
Confidential – file Nirdlinger

With regard to your proposal to put Agent Huff under surveillance for his connection with the Nirdlinger case, I disagree absolutely. Naturally, in this case as in all cases of its kind, the agent is automatically under suspicion, and I have not neglected to take necessary steps with regard to Huff. All his statements check closely with the facts and with our records, as well as with the dead man's records. I have even checked, without his knowledge, his whereabouts the night of the crime, and find he was at home all night. This in my opinion lets him out. A man of his experience can hardly fail to know if we attempt to watch his movements, and

we should thus lose the chance of his cheerful coopera-
tion on this case, which so far has been valuable, and
may become imperative. I point out to you further, his
record which has been exceptional in cases of fraud. I
strongly recommend that this whole idea be dropped.

Respectfully

I lifted the needle and ran it over again. It did things to
me. I don't only mean it was a relief. It made my heart
feel funny.

But then, after some more routine stuff, came this:

Confidential – file Nordlinger

SUMMARY – investigators' verbal reports for week
ending June 17th:

Daughter Lola Nirdlinger moved out of home June 8,
took up residence in two-room apartment, the Lycee
Arms, Yucca Street. No surveillance deemed necessary.

Widow remained at home until June 8, when she took
automobile ride, stopped at drugstore, made phone call,
took ride two succeeding days, stopped markets and
store selling women's gowns.

Night of June 11, man caller arrived at house 8:35, left
11:48. Description: – Tall, dark – age twenty-six or -
seven. Calls repeated June 12, 13, 14, 16. Man followed
night of first visit, identity ascertained as Beniamino
Sachetti, Lilac Court Apartments, North La Brea Avenue.

I was afraid to have Lola come down to the office any
more. But finding out they had no men assigned to her
meant that I could take her out somewhere. I called her
up and asked her if she would go with me to dinner. She
said she would like it more than anything she could
think of. I took her down to the Miramar at Santa

Monica. I said it would be nice to eat where we could see the ocean, but the real reason was I didn't want to take her to any place downtown, where I might run into somebody I knew.

We talked along during dinner about where she went to school, and why she didn't go to college, and a whole lot of stuff. It was kind of feverish, because we were both under a strain, but we got along all right. It was like she said. We both felt easy around each other somehow. I didn't say anything about what she had told me, last time, until we got in the car after dinner and started up the ocean for a ride. Then I brought it up myself.

'I thought over what you told me.'

'Can I say something?'

'Go ahead.'

'I've had it out with myself about that. I've thought it all over, and come to the conclusion I was wrong. It's very easy when you love somebody terribly, and then suddenly they're gone from you, to think it's somebody's fault. Especially when it's somebody you don't like. I don't like Phyllis. I guess it's partly jealousy. I was devoted to my mother. I was almost as devoted to my father. And then when he married Phyllis – I don't know, it seemed as though something had happened that couldn't happen. And then – these thoughts. What I felt instinctively when my mother died became a dead certainty when my father married Phyllis. I thought that showed why she did it. And it became a double certainty when this happened. But I haven't a thing to go on, have I? It's been terribly hard to make myself realize that, but I have. I've given up the whole idea, and I wish you'd forget that I ever told you.'

'I'm glad, in a way.'

'I guess you think I'm terrible.'

'I thought it over. I thought it over carefully, and all the more carefully because it would be most important for my company if they knew it. But there's nothing to go on. It's only a suspicion. That's all you have to tell.'

'I told you. I haven't even got that any more.'

'What you would tell the police, if you told them anything, is already a matter of public record. Your mother's death, your father's death – you haven't anything to add to what they already know. Why tell them?'

'Yes, I know.'

'If I were you, I would do nothing.'

'You agree with me then? That I haven't anything to go on?'

'I do.'

That ended that. But I had to find out about this Sachetti, and find out without her knowing I was trying to find out.

'Tell me something. What happened between you and Sachetti?'

'I told you. I don't want to talk about him.'

'How did you come to meet him?'

'Through Phyllis.'

'Through—?'

'His father was a doctor. I think I told you she used to be a nurse. He called on her, about joining some association that was being formed. But then when he got interested in me, he wouldn't come to the house. And then, when Phyllis found out I was meeting him, she told my father the most awful stories about him. I was

94

supposed not to meet him, but I did. There was something back of it, I knew that. But I never found out what it was, until—'

'Go on. Until what?'

'I don't want to go on. I told you I gave up any idea that there might be something—'

'Until what?'

'Until my father died. And then, quite suddenly, he didn't seem interested in me any more. He—'

'Yes?'

'He's going with Phyllis.'

'And—?'

'Can't you see what I thought? Do you have to make me say it? . . . I thought maybe they did it. I thought his going with me was just a blind for – something, I didn't know what. Seeing her, maybe. In case they got caught.'

'I thought he was with you – that night.'

'He was supposed to be. There was a dance over at the university, and I went over. I was to meet him there. But he got sick, and sent word he couldn't come. I got on a bus and went to a picture show. I never told anybody that.'

'What do you mean, sick?'

'He did have a cold, I know that. A dreadful cold. But – please don't make me talk any more about it. I've tried to put it out of my mind. I'm getting so I can believe it isn't true. If he wants to see Phyllis, it's none of my business. I mind. I wouldn't be telling the truth if I said I didn't mind. But – it's his privilege. Just because he does that is no reason for me to – think this of him. That wouldn't be right.'

'We won't talk about it any more.'

I stared into the darkness some more that night. I had killed a man, for money and a woman. I didn't have the money and I didn't have the woman. The woman was a killer out-and-out, and she had made a fool of me. She had used me for a cat's paw so she could have another man, and she had enough on me to hang me higher than a kite. If the man was in on it, there were two of them that could hang me. I got to laughing, a hysterical cackle, there in the dark. I thought about Lola, how sweet she was, and the awful thing I had done to her. I began subtracting her age from my age. She was nineteen, I'm thirty-four. That made a difference of fifteen years. Then I got to thinking that if she was nearly twenty, that would make a difference of only fourteen years. All of a sudden I sat up and turned on the light. I knew what that meant.

I was in love with her.

10

Right on top of that, Phyllis filed her claim. Keyes denied liability, on the ground that accident hadn't been proved. Then she filed suit, through the regular lawyer that had always handled her husband's business. She called me about half a dozen times, always from a drugstore, and I told her what to do. I had got so I felt sick the minute I heard her voice, but I couldn't take any chances. I told her to be ready, that they would try to prove something besides suicide. I didn't give her all of it, what they were thinking and what they were doing, but I let her know that murder was one of the things they would cover anyway, so she had better be ready for it when she went on the stand. It didn't faze her any. She seemed to have almost forgotten that there was a murder, and acted like the company was playing her some kind of a dirty trick in not paying her right away. That suited me fine. It was a funny sidelight on human nature, and especially on a woman's nature, but it was just exactly the frame of mind I would want her in to face a lot of corporation lawyers. If she stuck to her story, even with all Keyes might have been able to dig up on her, I still didn't see how she could miss.

That all took about a month, and the suit was to come up for trial in the early fall. All during that month, three or four nights a week, I was seeing Lola. I would call for her, at the little apartment house where she was living, and we would go to dinner, and then for a drive. She had got a little car, but we generally went in mine. I had gone completely nuts about her. Having it hanging over me all the time, what I had done to her, and how awful it would be if she ever found out, that had something to do with it, but it wasn't all. There was something so sweet about her, and we got along so nice, I mean we felt so happy when we were together. Anyway I did. She did too, I knew that. But then one night something happened. We were parked on the ocean road, about three miles above Santa Monica. They have places where you can park and sit and look. We were sitting there, watching the moon come up over the ocean. That sounds funny, don't it, that you can watch the moon come up over the Pacific Ocean? You can, just the same. The coast here runs almost due east and west, and when the moon comes up, off to your left, it's pretty as a picture. As soon as it lifted out of the sea, she slipped her hand into mine. I took it, but she took it away, quick.

'I mustn't do that.'

'Why not?'

'Lots of reasons. It's not fair to you, for one.'

'Did you hear me squawk?'

'You do like me, don't you?'

'I'm crazy about you.'

'I'm pretty crazy about you too, Walter. I don't know what I'd have done without you these last few weeks. Only—'

'Only what?'

'Are you sure you want to hear? It may hurt you.'

'Better hear it than guess at it.'

'It's about Nino.'

'Yes?'

'I guess he still means a lot to me.'

'Have you seen him?'

'No.'

'You'll get over it. Let me be your doctor. I'll guarantee a cure. Just give me a little time, and I'll promise to have you all right.'

'You're a nice doctor. Only—'

'Another "only"?'

'I *did* see him.'

'Oh.'

'No, I was telling the truth just now. I haven't talked with him. He doesn't know I've seen him. Only—'

'You sure have a lot of "only's."'

'Walter—'

She was getting more and more excited, and trying not to let me see it.

'—He didn't do it!'

'No?'

'This is going to hurt you terribly, Walter. I can't help it. You may as well know the truth. I followed them last night. Oh, I've followed them a lot of times, I've been insane. Last night, though, was the first time I ever got a chance to hear what they were saying. They went up to the Lookout and parked, and I parked down below, and crept up behind them. Oh, it was horrible enough. He told her he had been in love with her from the first, but felt it was hopeless – until this happened. But that wasn't all. They talked about money. He's spent all of that you let him have, and still he hasn't got his degree. He paid for his dissertation, but the rest he spent on her. And he was talking about where he'd get more. Listen, Walter—'

'Yes?'

'If they had done this together, she'd have to let him have money, wouldn't she?'

'Looks like it.'

'They never even mentioned anything about her letting him have money. My heart began to beat when I realized what that meant. And then they talked some more. They were there about an hour. They talked about lots of things, and I could tell, from what they said, that he wasn't in on it, and didn't know anything about it. I could tell! Walter, do you realize what that means? *He didn't do it!*'

She was so excited her fingers felt like steel, where they were clutched around my arm. I couldn't follow her. I could see that she meant something, something a whole lot more important than that Sachetti was innocent.

'I don't quite get it, Lola. I thought you had given up the idea that *anybody* was in on it.'

'I'll never give it up! . . . Yes, I did give it up, or try to. But that was only because I thought if there was something like that, *he* must have been in on it, and that would have been too terrible. If he had anything to do with it, I knew it couldn't be that. I *had* to know it, to believe it. But now – oh no, Walter, I haven't given it up. She did it, somehow. I know it. And now, I'll get her. I'll get her for it, if it's the last thing I do.'

'How?'

'She's suing you company, isn't she? She even has the nerve to do that. All right. You tell your company not to worry. I'll come and sit right alongside of you, Walter. I'll tell them what to ask her. I'll tell them—'

'Wait a minute, Lola, wait a minute—'

'I'll tell them everything they need to know. I told you there was plenty more, besides what I told you. I'll tell them to ask her about the time I came in on her, in her bedroom, with some kind of foolish red silk thing on her, that looked like a shroud or something, with her face all smeared up with white powder and red lipstick, with a dagger in her hand, making faces at herself in front of a mirror – oh yes, I'll tell them to ask her about that. I'll tell them to ask her why she was down in a boulevard store, a week before my father died, pricing black dresses. That's something she doesn't know I know. I went in there about five minutes after she left. The saleslady was just putting the frocks away. She was telling me what lovely numbers they were, only she couldn't understand why Mrs Nirdlinger would be considering them, because they were really mourning. That was one reason I wanted my father to take that trip, so I could get him out of the house and find out what she was up to. I'll tell them—'

'But wait a minute, Lola. You can't do that. Why – they can't ask her such things as that—'

'If they can't, I can! I'll stand right up in court and yell them at her. I'll be heard! No judge, no policeman, or *anybody* – can stop me. I'll force it out of her if I have to go up there and choke it out of her. *I'll make her tell! I'll not be stopped!*'

11

I don't know when I decided to kill Phyllis. It seemed to me that ever since that night, somewhere in the back of my head I had known I would have to kill her, for what she knew about me, and because the world isn't big enough for two people once they've got something like that on each other. But I know when I decided *when* to kill her, and *where* to kill her and *how* to kill her. It was right after that night when I was watching the moon come up over the ocean with Lola. Because the idea that Lola would put on an act like that in the courtroom, and that then Phyllis would lash out and tell her the truth, that was too horrible for me to think about. Maybe I haven't explained it right, yet, how I felt about this girl Lola. It wasn't anything like what I had felt for Phyllis. That was some kind of unhealthy excitement that came over me just at the sight of her. This wasn't anything like that. It was just a sweet peace that came over me as soon as I was with her, like when we would drive along for an hour without saying a word, and then she would look up at me and we still didn't have to say anything. I hated what I had done, and it kept sweeping over me that if there was any way I could make sure she would never find out, why then maybe I could marry her, and forget the whole thing, and be happy with her the rest of my life. There was only one way I could be sure, and that was to get rid of anybody that knew. What she told me about Sachetti showed there was only one I had to get rid of, and that was Phyllis. And the rest of what she told me, about what she was going to do, meant I had to move quick, before that suit came to trial.

I wasn't going to leave it so Sachetti could come back and take her away from me, though. I was going to do it so he would be put in a spot. Police are hard to fool, but Lola would never be quite sure he hadn't done it. And of course if he did one, so far as she was concerned he probably did the other.

My next day at the finance company, I put through a lot of routine stuff, sent the file clerk out on an errand, and took out the folder on Sachetti. I slipped it in my desk. In that folder was a key to his car. In our finance company, just to avoid trouble in case of a repossess, we make every borrower deposit the key to his car along with the other papers on his loan, and of course Sachetti had had to do the same. That was back in the winter when he took out the loan on his car. I slipped the key out of its envelope, and when I went out to lunch I had a duplicate made. When I got back I sent the file clerk on another errand, put the original key back in its envelope, and returned the folder to the file. That was what I wanted. I had the key to his car, and nobody there even knew I had the folder out of the file.

*

Next I had to get hold of Phyllis, but I didn't dare ring her. I had to wait till she called. I sat around the house three nights, and the fourth night the phone rang.

'Phyllis, I've got to see you.'

'It's about time.'

'You know the reason I haven't. Now get this. We've got to meet, to go over things in connection with this suit – and after that, I don't think we have anything to fear.'

'Can we meet? I thought you said—'

'That's right. They've been watching you. But I found out something today. They've cut down the detail assigned to you to one shift, and he goes off at eleven.'

'What's that?'

'They did have these men assigned to you, in shifts, but they weren't finding out very much, so they thought they'd cut down the expense, and now they've only got one. He goes on in the afternoon, and goes off at eleven o'clock, unless there's something to hold him. We'll have to meet after that.'

'All right. Then come up to the house—'

'Oh no, we can't take a chance like that. But we can meet. Tomorrow night, around midnight, you sneak out. Take the car and sneak out. If anybody drops in the evening, get rid of them well before eleven o'clock. Get rid of them, turn out all lights, have the place looking like you had gone to bed well before this man goes off. So he'll have no suspicions whatever.'

The reason for that was that if Sachetti was going to be with her the next night, I wanted him to be well out of there and home in bed, long before I was to meet her. I had to have his car, and I didn't want the connections to be so close I had to wait. The rest of it was all hooey, about the one shift I mean. I wanted her to think she could meet me safely. As to whether they had one shift on her, or three, or six, I didn't know and I didn't care. If somebody followed her, so much the better, for what I had to do. They'd have to move fast to catch me, and if they saw her deliberately knocked off, why that would be just that much more Mr Sachetti would have to explain when they caught up with him.

'Lights out by eleven.'

'Lights out, the cat out, and the place locked up.'

'All right, where do I meet you?'

'Meet me in Griffith Park, a couple of hundred yards up Riverside from Los Feliz. I'll be parked there, and we'll take a ride, and talk it over. Don't park on Los Feliz. Park in among the trees, in the little glade near the bridge. Park where I can see you, and walk over.'

'In between the two streets?'

'That's it. Make it twelve-thirty sharp. I'll be a minute or two ahead of time, so you can hop right in and you won't have to wait.'

'Twelve-thirty, two hundred yards up Riverside.'

'That's right. Close your garage door when you come out, so anybody passing won't notice the car's out.'

'I'll be there, Walter.'

'Oh, and one other thing. I traded my car in since I saw you. I've got another one.' I told her the make. 'It's a small dark-blue coupe. You can't miss it.'

'A blue coupe?'

'Yes.'

'That's funny.'

I knew why it was funny. She'd been riding around in

a blue coupe for the last month, the same one if she only knew it, but I didn't tumble. 'Yeah, I guess it's funny at that, me driving around in an oil can, but the big car was costing too much. I had a chance for a deal on this one, so I took it.'

'It's the funniest thing I ever heard.'

'Why?'

'Oh – nothing. Tomorrow night at twelve-thirty.'

'Twelve-thirty.'

'I'm just dying to see you.'

'Same here.'

'Well – I had something to talk to you about, but I'll let it wait till tomorrow. Good-bye.'

'Good-bye.'

When she hung up I got the paper and checked the shows in town. There was a downtown theater that had a midnight show, and the bill was to hold over the whole week. That was what I wanted. I drove down there. It was about ten-thirty when I got in, and I sat in the balcony, so I wouldn't be seen by the downstairs ushers. I watched the show close, and paid attention to the gags, because it was to be part of my alibi next night that I had been there. In the last sequence of the feature I saw an actor I knew. He played the part of a waiter, and I had once sold him a hunk of life insurance, $7,000 for an endowment policy, all paid up when he bought it. His name was Jack Christolf. That helped me. I stayed till the show was out, and looked at my watch. It was 12:48.

Next day around lunch time I called up Jack Christolf. They said he was at the studio and I caught him there. 'I hear you knocked them for a loop in this new one, "Gun Play."'

'I didn't do bad. Did you see it?'

'No, I want to catch it. Where's it playing?'

He named five theaters. He knew them all. 'I'm going to drop in on it the very first chance I get. Well say old man, how about another little piece of life insurance? Something to do with all this dough you're making.'

'I don't know. I don't know. To tell you the truth, I might be interested. Yes, I might.'

'When can I see you?'

'Well, I'm busy this week. I don't finish up here till Friday, and I thought I would go away for a rest over the weekend. But next week, any time.'

'How about at night?'

'Well, we might do that.'

'How about tomorrow night?'

'I tell you. Ring me home tomorrow night, around dinner time, some time around seven o'clock. I'll let you know then. If I can make it, I'll be glad to see you.'

That would be why I went to that particular picture tonight, that I had to talk to this actor tomorrow night, and I wanted to see his picture, so I could talk about it and make him feel good.

About four o'clock I drove up through Griffith Park, and checked it over close, what I was going to do. I picked a spot for my car, and a spot for Sachetti's car. They weren't far apart, but the spot for my car was close to one end of the bridle path, where they ride horses in the daytime. It winds all over the hills there, but right above this place it comes out on the automobile road up

107

above. I mean, up high in the hills. This park, they call it a park, but it's really a scenic drive, up high above Hollywood and the San Fernando Valley, for people in cars, and a hilly ride for people on horses. People on foot don't go there much. What I was going to do was let her get in and then start up the hill. When I came to one of those platforms where the road is graded to a little flat place so people can park and look over the valley, I was going to pull in, and say something about parking there, so we could talk. Only I wasn't to park. The car was accidentally on purpose, going to roll over the edge, and I was going to jump. As soon as I jumped I was going to dive into the bridle path, race on down to my car, and drive home. From where I was going to park Sachetti's car to where I was going to run her over the edge was about two miles, by road. But by bridle path it was only a hundred yards, on account of the road winding all through the hills for an easy grade, and the bridle path being almost straight up and down. Less than a minute after the crash, before even a crowd could get there, I would be away and gone.

I drove up the hill and picked the place. It was one of the little lookouts, with room for just one or two cars, not one of the big ones. The big ones have stone parapets around them. This one didn't have any. I got out and looked down. There was a drop of at least two hundred feet, straight, and probably another hundred feet after that where the car would roll after it struck. I practised what I was going to do. I ran up to the edge, threw the gear in neutral, and pushed open the door. I made a note I would only half close my door when she got in, so I could open it quick. There was a chance she would grab the emergency as the car went over and save herself, and then have the drop on me. There was a chance I wouldn't jump clear, and that I would go over the edge with her. That was OK. On this, you have to take a chance. I ate dinner alone, at a big downtown seafood house. The waiter knew me. I made a gag with him, to fix it on his mind it was Friday. When I finished I went back to the office and told Joe Pete I had to work. I stayed till ten o'clock. He was down at his desk, reading a detective story magazine when I went out.

'You're working late, Mr Huff.'

'Yeah, and I'm not done yet.'

'Working home?'

'No, I got to see a picture. There's a ham by the name of Jack Christolf I've got to talk to tomorrow night, and I've got to see his picture. He might not like it if I didn't. No time for it tomorrow. I've got to catch it tonight.'

'They sure do love theirself, them actors.'

I parked near the theater, loafed around, and around eleven o'clock I went in. I bought a downstairs seat this time. I took a program and put it in my pocket. I checked, it had the date on it. I still had to talk with an usher, fix it on her mind what day it was, and pull something so she would remember me. I picked the one on the door, not the one in the aisle inside. I wanted enough light so that she could see me well.

'Is the feature on?'

'No sir, it's just finished. It goes on again at 11:20.'

I knew that. That was why I had gone in at 11 o'clock instead of sooner. 'Holy smoke, that's a long time to wait ... Is Christolf in all of it?'

'I think only in the last part, sir.'

'You mean I've got to wait till one o'clock in the morning to see that ham?'

'It'll be on tomorrow night too, sir, if you don't care to wait so long tonight. They'll refund your money at the box office for you.'

'Tomorrow night? Let's see, tomorrow's Saturday, isn't it?'

'Yes sir.'

'Nope, can't make it. Got to see it tonight.'

I had that much of it. Next I had to pull something so she would remember me. It was a hot night, and she had the top button of her uniform unbuttoned. I reached up there, and buttoned it, quick. I took her by surprise.

'You ought to be more careful.'

'Listen, big boy, do I have to drip sweat off the end of my nose, just to please you?'

She unbuttoned it again. I figured she would remember it. I went in.

As soon as the aisle usher showed me a seat, I moved once, to the other side of the house. I sat there a minute, and then I slipped out, through a side exit. Later, I would say I stayed for the end of the show. I had my talk with Christolf, for a reason for being there late. I had my talk with Joe Pete, and his log would prove what day it was. I had the usher. I couldn't prove I was there clear to the end, but no alibi ought to be perfect. This was as good a one as most juries hear, and a whole lot better than most. As far as I could go with it, it certainly didn't sound like a man that was up to murder.

I got in the car and drove straight to Griffith Park.

That time of night I could make time. When I got there I looked at my watch. It was 11:24. I parked, cut the motor, took the key and turned off the lights. I walked over to Los Feliz, and from there down to Hollywood Boulevard. It's about half a mile. I legged it right along, and got to the boulevard at 11:35. I boarded a street car and took a seat up front. When we got to La Brea it was five minutes to twelve. So far, my timing was perfect.

I got off the car and walked down to the Lilac Court Apartments, where Sachetti lived. It's one of those court places where they have a double row of bungalows off a center lane, one-room shacks mostly that rent for about $3 a week. I went in the front. I didn't want to come up to the park from outside where I would look like a snooper if anybody saw me. I walked right in the front, and down past his bungalow. I knew the number. It was No. 11. There was a light inside. That was OK. That was just like I wanted it.

I marched straight through, back to the auto court in the rear, where the people that live there keep their cars. Anyway, those of them that have cars. There was a colllection of second-, third-, fourth-, and ninth-hand wrecks out there, and sure enough right in the middle was his. I got in, shoved the key in the ignition and started it. I cut on the lights and started to back. A car pulled in from the outside. I turned my head so I couldn't be seen in the headlights, and backed on out. I drove up to Hollywood Boulevard. It was exactly twelve o'clock. I checked his gas. He had plenty.

I took it easy, but still it was only 12:18 when I got back to Griffith Park. I drove up into Glendale, because I didn't want to be more than two or three minutes ahead of time. I thought about Sachetti and how he was going to make out with his alibi. He didn't have one, because that's the worst alibi in the world to be home in bed, unless you've got some way to prove it, with phone calls or something. He didn't have any way to prove it. He didn't even have a phone.

Just past the railroad tracks I turned, came on back, went up Riverside a little way, turned facing Los Feliz, and parked. I cut the motor and the lights. It was exactly 12:27. I turned around and looked, and saw my own car, about a hundred yards back of me. I looked into the little glade. No car was parked there. She hadn't come.

I held my watch in my hand. The hand crept around to 12:30. Still she hadn't come. I put my watch back in my pocket. A twig cracked – off in the bushes. I jumped. Then I wound down the window on the right hand side of the car, and sat there looking off in the bushes to see what it was. I must have stared out there at least a minute. Another twig cracked, closer this time. Then there was a flash, and something hit me in the chest like Jack Dempsey had hauled off and given me all he had. There was a shot. I knew then what had happened to me. I wasn't the only one that figured the world wasn't big enough for two people, when they knew that about each other. I had come there to kill her, but she had beaten me to it.

I fell back on the seat, and I heard footsteps running away. There I was, with a bullet through my chest, in a stolen car, and the owner of the car the very man that Keyes had been tailing for the last month and a half. I pulled myself up by the wheel. I reached up for the key, then remembered I had to leave it in there. I opened the door. I could feel the sweat start out on my head from what it took out of me to turn the handle. I got out, somehow. I began staggering up the road to my car. I couldn't walk straight. I wanted to sit down, to ease that awful weight on my chest, but I knew if I did that I'd never get there. I rememberd I had to get the car key ready, and took it out of my pocket. I got there and climbed in. I shoved the key in and pulled the starter. That was the last I knew *that* night.

12

don't know if you've ever been under ether. You come out of it a little bit at a time. First a kind of a gray light shines on one part of your mind, just a dim gray light, and then it gets bigger, but slow. All the time it's getting bigger you're trying to gag the stuff out of your lungs. It sounds like an awful groan, like you were in pain or something, but that's not it. You try to gag it out of your lungs, and you make those sounds to try and force it out. But away inside somewhere your head is working all the time. You know where you're at, and even if all kind of cock-eyed ideas do swim through the gray light, the main part of you is there, and you can think, maybe not so good, but a little bit.

It seemed to me I had been thinking, even before I began to come to. I knew there must be somebody with me there, but I didn't know who it was. I could hear them talking, but it wouldn't quite reach me what they were saying. Then I could hear it. It was a woman, telling me to open my mouth for a little ice, that would make me feel better. I opened my mouth. I got the ice. I figured the woman must be a nurse. Still I didn't know who else was there. I thought a long time, then figured it out I would open my eyes just a little bit and close them quick, and see who was in the room. I did that. At first I couldn't see anything. It was a hospital room, and there was a table pushed up near the bed, with a lot of stuff on it. It was broad daylight. Over my chest the covers were piled high, so that meant a lot of bandages. I opened my eyes a little bit further and peeped around. The nurse was sitting beside the table watching me. But over back of her was somebody. I had to wait till she moved to see who it was, but I knew anyway even without seeing.

It was Keyes.

It must have been an hour that I lay there after that, and never opened my eyes at all. I was all there in the head by that time. I tried to think. I couldn't. Every time I tried to gag more ether out, there would come this stab of pain in my chest. That was from the bullet. I quit trying to gag out the ether then and the nurse began talking to me. She knew. Pretty soon I had to answer her. Keyes walked over.

'Well, that theater program saved you.'

'Yeah?'

'That double wad of paper wasn't much, but it was enough. You'll bleed a little bit for a while where that bullet grazed your lung, but you're lucky it wasn't your heart. Another eighth of an inch, and it would have been curtains for you.'

'They get the bullet?'

'Yeah.'

'They get the woman?'

'Yeah.'

I didn't say anything. I thought it was curtains for me anyway, but I just lay there. 'They got her, and I got plenty to tell you boy. This thing is a honey. But give me a half hour. I got to go out and get some breakfast. Maybe you'll be feeling better then yourself.'

He went. He didn't act like I was in any trouble, or he was sore at me, or anything like that. I couldn't figure it out. In a couple of minutes an orderly came in 'You got any papers in this hospital?'

'Yes sir, I think I can get you one.'

He came back with a paper and found it for me. He knew what I wanted. It wasn't on Page 1. It was in the second section where they print the local news that's not quite hot enough to go on the front page. This was it:

MYSTERY SHROUDS
GRIFFITH PARK
SHOOTING
Two Held After Walter Huff, Insurance Man, Is Found Wounded at Wheel of Car on Riverside Drive After Midnight

Police are investigating the circumstances surrounding the shooting of Walter Huff, an insurance man living in the Los Feliz Hills, who was found unconscious at the wheel of his car in Griffith Park shortly after midnight last night, a bullet wound in his chest. Two persons were held pending a report on Huff's condition today. They are:

Lola Nirdlinger, 19.

Beniamino Sachetti, 26.

Miss Nirdlinger gave her address as the Lycee Arms Apartments, Yucca Street, and Sachetti as the Lilac Court Apartments, La Brea Avenue.

Huff apparently was shot as he was driving along Riverside Drive from the direction of Burbank. Police arriving at the scene shortly afterward found Miss Nirdlinger and Sachetti at the car trying to get him out. A short distance away was a pistol with one chamber discharged. Both denied responsibility for the shooting but refused to make any further statement.

They brought me orange juice and I lay there trying to figure that out. You think I fell for it, do you? That I thought Lola had shot me, or Sachetti maybe, out of jealousy, something like that? I did not. I knew who shot me. I knew who I had a date with, who knew I was going to be there, who wanted me out of the way. Nothing could change me on that. But what were these two doing there? I pounded on it awhile, and I couldn't make any sense out of it, except a little piece of it. Of course Lola was following Sachetti again that night, or thought she was. That explained what she was doing there. But what was he doing there? None of it made sense. And all the while I kept having this numb feeling that I was sunk, and not only sunk for what I had done, but for what Lola was going to find out. That was the worst.

It was almost noon before Keyes came back. He saw the paper. He pulled up a chair near the bed. 'I've been down to the office.'

'Yeah?'

'It's been a wild morning. A wild morning on top of a wild night.'

'What's going on?'

'Now I'll tell you something you don't know. This Sachetti, Huff, this same Sachetti that plugged you last night, is the same man we've been tailing for what he might know about that other thing. That Nirdlinger case.'

'You don't mean it.'

'I do mean it. I started to tell you, you remember, but Norton got these ideas about keeping all that stuff confidential from agents, so I didn't. That's it. The same man, Huff. Did I tell you? Did I tell Norton? Did I say there was something funny about that case?'

'What else?'

'Plenty. Your finance company called up.'

'Yeah?'

'They popped out with what we'd have known in the first place, I mean me and Norton, if we had taken you into our confidence completely from the beginning. If you had known about this Sachetti, you could have told us what we just found out today, and it's the key to the whole case.'

'He got a loan.'

'That's right. He got a loan. But that's not it. That's not the important thing. *He was in your office the day you delivered that policy to Nirdlinger.*'

'I couldn't be certain.'

'We are. We checked it all up, with Nettie, with the finance company records, with the records in the policy department. He was in there, and the girl was in there, and that's what we've been waiting for. That gives it to us, the hook-up we never had before.'

'What do you mean, hook-up?'

'Listen, we know Nirdlinger never told his family about this policy. We know that from a check we've made with the secretary. He never told anybody. Just the same the family *knew* about it, didn't they?'

'Well – I don't know.'

'They knew. They didn't put him on the spot for nothing. They knew, and now we know *how* they knew. This ties it up.'

'Any court would assume they knew.'

'I'm not a court. I'm talking about for my own satisfaction, for my own knowledge that I'm right. Because look, Huff, I might demand an investigation on the basis of what my instinct tells me. But I don't go into a courtroom and go to bat with it without knowing. And now I know. What's more, this ties the girl in.'

'The – who?'

'The girl. The daughter. She was there, too. In your office, I mean. Oh yeah, you may think it funny, that a girl would pull something like that on her own father. But it's happened. It's happened plenty of times. For fifty thousand bucks it's going to happen plenty of times again.'

'I – don't believe that.'

'You will, before I get done. Now listen Huff. I'm still shy something. I'm shy one link. They put you on the spot for something you could testify to when this suit comes up, I can see that. But what?'

'What do you mean, what?'

'What is it you know about them they would knock you off for? Their being in your office, that's not enough. There must be something else. Now what is it?'

'I – don't know. I can't think of anything.'

'There's something. Maybe it's something you've forgotten about, something that doesn't mean anything to you but is important to them. Now what is it?'

'There's nothing. There *can't* be.'

'There's something. There must be.'

He was walking around now. I could feel the bed shake from his weight. 'Keep it on your mind, Huff. We've got a few days. Try to think what it is.'

He lit a cigarette, and pounded around some more. 'That's the beauty of this, we've got a few days. You can't appear at a hearing until next week at the earliest, and that gives us what we need. A little help from the cops, a few treatments with the rubber hose, something like that, and sooner or later this pair is going to spill it. Especially that girl. She'll crack before long ... Believe me this is what we've been waiting for. It's tough on you, but now we've got them where we can really throw the works into them. Oh yeah, this is a real break. We'll clean this case up now. Before night, with luck.'

I closed my eyes. I couldn't think of anything but Lola, a lot of cops around her, maybe beating her up, trying to make her spill something that she knew no more about than the man in the moon. Her face jumped in front of me and all of a sudden something hit it in the mouth, and it started to bleed.

'Keyes.'

'Yeah?'

'There was something. Now you speak of it.'

'I'm listening boy.'

'I killed Nirdlinger.'

13

He sat there staring at me. I had told him everything he needed to know, even about Lola. It seemed funny it had only taken about ten minutes. Then he got up. I grabbed him.

'Keyes.'

'I've got to go, Huff.'

'See that they don't beat her.'

'I've got to go now. I'll be back after a while.'

'Keyes, if you let them beat her, I'll – kill you. You've got it all now. I've told you, and I've told you for one reason and one reason only. It's so they won't beat her. You've got to promise me that. You owe me that much Keyes—'

He shook my hand off and left.

While I was telling him I hoped for some kind of peace when I got done. It had been bottled up in me a long time. I had been sleeping with it, dreaming about it, breathing with it. I didn't get any peace. The only thing I could think of was Lola, and how she was going to find out about it at last, and know me for what I was.

*

About three o'clock the orderly came in with the afternoon papers. They didn't have any of what I had told Keyes. But they had been digging into their files, after the morning story, and they had it about the first Mrs Nirdlinger's death, and Nirdlinger's death, and now me being shot. A woman feature writer had got in out there and talked with Phyllis. It was she that called it the House of Death, and put in about those blood-red drapes. Once I saw that stuff I knew it wouldn't be long. That meant even a dumb cluck of a woman reporter could see there was something funny out there.

It was half past eight that night before Keyes came back. He shooed out the nurse as soon as he came in the room, and then went out a minute. When he came back he had Norton with him, and a man named Keswick that was a corporation lawyer they called in on big cases, and Shapiro, the regular head of the legal department. They all stood around, and it was Norton that started to speak. 'Huff.'

'Yes sir.'

'Have you told anybody about this?'

'Nobody but Keyes.'

'Nobody else?'

'Not a soul ... God, no.'

'There have been no policemen here?'

'They've been here. I saw them out in the hall. I guess it was me they were whispering about. The nurse wouldn't let them in.'

They all looked at each other. 'Then I guess we can begin. Keyes, perhaps you had better explain it to him.'

Keyes opened his mouth to say something, but

Keswick shut him up, and got Norton into a corner. Then they called Keyes over. Then they called Shapiro. I could catch a word, now and then. It was some kind of a proposition they were going to make to me, and it was a question of whether they were all going to be witnesses. Keswick was for the proposition, but he didn't want anybody to be able to say he had been in on it. They finally settled it that Keyes would make it on his own personal responsibility, and the rest of them wouldn't be there. Then they all tiptoed out. They didn't even say good-bye. It was funny. They didn't act like I had played them or the company any particularly dirty trick. They acted like I was some kind of an animal that had an awful sore on his face, and they didn't even want to look at it.

After they left Keyes sat down. 'This is an awful thing you've done, Huff.'

'I know it.'

'I guess there's no need my saying more about that part.'

'No, no need.'

'I'm sorry. I've – kind of liked you, Huff.'

'I know. Same here.'

'I don't often like somebody. At my trade, you can't afford to. The whole human race looks – a little bit crooked.'

'I know. You trusted me, and I let you down.'

'Well – we won't talk about it.'

'There's nothing to say ... Did you see her?'

'Yes. I saw them all. Him, her, and the wife.'

'What did she say?'

'Nothing ... I didn't tell her, you see. I let her do the talking. She thinks Sachetti shot you.'

'For what?'

'Jealousy.'

'Oh.'

'She's upset about you. But when she found out you weren't badly hurt she—. Well, she—'

'—Was glad of it.'

'In a way. She tried not to be. But she felt that it proved Sachetti loved her. She couldn't help it.'

'I see.'

'She was worried about you, though. She likes you.'

'Yeah. I know. She ... likes me.'

'She was following you. She thought you were him. That was all there was to that.'

'I figured that out.'

'I talked to *him*.'

'Oh yeah, you told me. What was he doing there?'

He did some more of his pounding around then. The night light over my head was the only light in the room. I could only half see him, but I could feel the bed shake when he marched.

'Huff, there's a story.'

'Yeah? How do you mean?'

'You just got yourself tangled up with an Irrawaddy cobra, that's all. That woman – it makes my blood run cold just to think of her. She's a pathological case, that's all. The worst I ever heard of.'

'A what?'

'They've got a name for it. You ought to read more of this modern psychology, Huff. I do. I wouldn't tell Norton. He'd think I was going highbrow or something. I find it helpful though. There's plenty of stuff in my field where it's the only thing that explains what they do. It's depressing, but it clears up things.'

'I still don't get it.'

'You will ... Sachetti wasn't in love with her.'

'No?'

'He's known her. Five or six years. His father was a doctor. He had a sanatorium up in the Verdugo Hills about a quarter mile from this place where she was head nurse.'

'Oh yeah. I remember about that.'

'Sachetti met her up there. Then one time the old man had some tough luck. Three children died on him.'

The old creepy feeling began to go up my back. He went on. 'They died of—'

'—Pneumonia.'

'You heard about it?'

'No. Go on.'

'Oh. You heard about the Arrowhead business.'

'Yes.'

'They died on him, and there was an awful time and the old man took the rap for it. Not with the police. They didn't find anything to concern them. But with the Department of Health and his clientele. It ruined him. He had to sell his place. Not long after that he died.'

'Pneumonia?'

'No. He was quite old. But Sachetti thought there was something funny about it, and he couldn't shake it out of his mind about this woman. She was over there too much, and she seemed to take too much interest in the children up there. He had nothing to go on, except some kind of a hunch. You follow me?'

'Go on.'

'He never did anything about it till the first Mrs Nirdlinger died. It happened that *one* of those children was related to that Mrs Nirdlinger, in such fashion that when that child died, Mrs Nirdlinger became executrix for quite a lot of property the child was due to inherit. In fact, as soon as the legal end was cleared up, Mrs Nirdlinger came into the property itself. Get that, Huff. That's the awful part. Just *one* of those children was mixed up with property.'

'How about the other two?'

'Nothing. Those two children died just to cover the trail up a little. Think of that, Huff. This woman would even kill two extra children, just to get the one child that she wanted, and mix things up so it would look like one of those cases of negligence they sometimes have in those hospitals. I tell you, she's a pathological case.'

'Go on.'

'When the first Mrs Nirdlinger died, Sachetti elected himself a one-man detective agency to find out what it was all about. He wanted to clear his father for one thing, and the woman had become an obsession with him for another thing. I don't mean he fell for her. I mean he just had to know the truth about her.'

'Yeah, I can see that.'

'He kept up his work at the university, as well as he could, and then he made a chance to get in there, and talk with her. He already knew her, so when he went up there with some kind of a proposition to join a physicians'-and-nurses' association that was being formed, he figured she wouldn't think anything of it. But then something happened. He met this girl, and it was a case of love at first sight, and then his fine scheme to get at the truth about the wife went on the rocks. He didn't want to make the girl unhappy, and he really had nothing to go on, so he called it off. He didn't want to go to the house after what he suspected about the wife, so he began meeting the girl outside. Just one little thing happened, though, to make him think that maybe he had been right. The wife, as soon as she found out what was going on, began telling Lola cock-eyed stories about him, and got the father to forbid Lola to see him. There was no reason for that, except that maybe this woman didn't want anything named Sachetti within a mile of her, after what happened. Do you follow this?'

'I follow it.'

'Then Nirdlinger got it. And suddenly Sachetti knew he had to go after this woman to mean it. He quit seeing Lola. He didn't even tell her why. He went up to this woman and began making love to her, as hard as he knew. That is, almost as hard as he knew. He figured, if it was her he was coming to see, she'd not forbid him to come, not at all. You see, she was Lola's guardian. But if Lola got married, the husband would be the guardian, and that would mix it all up on the property. You see—'

'Lola was next.'

'That's it. After she got you out of the way for what you knew about her, Lola was next. Of course at this time Sachetti didn't know anything about you, but he did know about Lola, or was pretty sure he knew.'

'Go on.'

'That brings us down to last night. Lola followed him. That is, she followed his car when you took it. She was turning into the parking lot when you pulled out.'

'I saw the car.'

'Sachetti went home early. The wife chased him out. He went to his room and started to go to bed, but he couldn't shake it out of his mind that something was going on that night. For one thing, being chased out looked funny. For another thing, the wife had asked him earlier in the day a couple of things about Griffith Park, when they closed the roads down there for the night, and which roads they closed – things that could only mean she had something cooking in that park late at night sometime, he didn't know when. So instead of going to bed, he decided to go up to her house and keep an eye on her. He went out to get his car. When he found it gone, he almost fainted, because Lola had a key to it. Don't forget, he knew Lola was next.'

'Go on.'

'He grabbed a cab and went down to Griffith Park. He began walking around blind – he didn't have any idea what was up, or even when to look. He started at the wrong place – at the far end of the little glade. Then he heard the shot. He ran over, and he and Lola got to you about the same time. He thought Lola was shot. She thought he was shot. When Lola saw who it was, she thought Sachetti shot him, and she was putting on an act about it when the police got there.'

'I get it now.'

'That woman, that wife, is an out-and-out lunatic. Sachetti told me he found five cases, all before the three little children, where patients died under her while she was a nurse, two of them where she got property out of it.'

'All of pneumonia?'

'Three. The other two were operative cases.'

'How did she do it?'

'Sachetti never found out. He thinks she found out some way to do it with the serum, combining with another drug. He wishes he could get it out of her. He thinks it would be important.'

'Well?'

'You're sunk, Huff.'

'I know it.'

'We had it out this afternoon. Down at the company. I had the whip hand. There was no two ways about it. I called it long ago, even when Norton was still talking suicide.'

'You did that all right.'

'I persuaded them the case ought never to come to trial.'

'You can't hush it up.'

'We can't hush it up, we know that. But having it come out that an agent of this company committed murder is one thing. Having it plastered all over every paper in the country for the two weeks of a murder trial is something else.'

'I see.'

'You're to give me a statement. You're to give me a statement setting forth every detail of what you did, and have a notary attest it. You're to mail it to me, registered. You're to do that Thursday of next week, so I get it Friday.'

'Next Thursday.'

'That's right. In the meantime, we hold everything, about this last shooting, I mean, because you're in no condition to testify at a hearing. Now get this. There'll be a reservation for you, under a name I'll give you, on a steamer leaving San Pedro Thursday night for Balboa and points south. You take that steamer. Friday I get your statement and at once turn it over to the police. That's the first I knew about it. That's why Norton and his friends left just now. There's no witnesses to this. It's a deal between you and me, and if you ever try to call it on me I'll deny it, and I'll prove there was no such deal. I've taken care of that.'

'I won't try.'

'As soon as we notify the police, we post a reward for your capture. And listen Huff, if you're ever caught, that reward will be paid, and you'll be tried, and if there's any way we can help it along, you're going to be hung. We don't want it brought to trial, but if it is brought to trial, we're going through with it to the hilt. Have you got that?'

'I've got it.'

'Before you get on that boat, you'll have to hand to me the registry receipt for that statement. I've got to know I've got it.'

'What about her?'

'Who?'

'Phyllis?'

'I've taken care of her.'

'There's just one thing, Keyes.'

'What is it?'

'I still don't know about that girl, Lola. You say you hold everything. I guess that means you hold her and Sachetti, pending the hearing. The hearing that's not going to be held. Well, listen. I've got to know no harm comes to her. I've got to have your solemn word on that, or you'll get no statement, and the case will come to

trial, and all the rest of it. I'll blow the whole ship out of
water. Do you get that, Keyes? What about her?'

'We hold Sachetti. He's consented to it.'

'Did you hear me? What about her?'

'She's out.'

'She's – what?'

'We bailed her out. It's a bailable offense. You didn't
die, you see.'

'Does she know about me?'

'No. I told you I told her nothing.'

He got up, looked at his watch, and tiptoed out in the
hall. I closed my eyes. Then I felt somebody near me. I
opened my eyes again. It was Lola.

'Walter.'

'Yes. Hello, Lola.'

'I'm terribly sorry.'

'I'm all right.'

'I didn't know Nino knew about us. He must have
found out. He didn't mean anything. But he's – hot-
tempered'

'You love him?'

'... Yes.'

'I just wanted to know.'

'I'm sorry that you feel as you do.'

'It's all right.'

'Can I ask something? That I haven't any right to
ask?'

'What is it?'

'That you do not prosecute. That you not appear
against him. You don't have to, do you?'

'I won't.'

'... Sometimes I almost love you, Walter.'

She sat looking at me, and all of a sudden she leaned over close. I turned my head away, quick. She looked hurt and sat there a long time. I didn't look at her. Some kind of peace came to me then at last. I knew I couldn't have her and never could have had her. I couldn't kiss the girl whose father I killed.

When she was at the door I said good-bye and wished her good luck, and then Keyes came back.

'OK on the statement, Keyes.'

'It's the best way.'

'OK on everything. Thanks.'

'Don't thank me.'

'I feel that way.'

'You've got no reason to thank me.' A funny look came in his eyes. 'I don't think they're going to catch up with you, Huff. I think – well maybe I'm doing you a favor at that. Maybe you'd rather have it that way.'

14

What you've just read, if you've read it, is the statement. It took me five days to write it, but at last, on Thursday afternoon, I got it done. That was yesterday. I sent it out by the orderly to be registered, and around five o'clock Keyes dropped by for the receipt. It'll be more than he bargained for, but I wanted to put it all down. Maybe she'll see it sometime, and not think so bad of me after she understands how it all was. Around seven o'clock I put on my clothes. I was weak, but I could walk. After a bite to eat I sent for a taxi and went down to the pier. I went to bed right away, and stayed there till early this afternoon. Then I couldn't stand it any longer, alone there in the stateroom, and went up on deck. I found my chair and sat there looking at the coast of Mexico, where we were going past it. But I had a funny feeling I wasn't going anywhere. I kept thinking about Keyes, and the look he had in his eye that day, and what he meant by what he said. Then, all of a sudden, I found out. I heard a little gasp beside me. Before I even looked I knew who it was. I turned to the next chair. It was Phyllis.

'You.'

'Hello, Phyllis.'

'Your man Keyes – he's quite a matchmaker.'

'Oh yeah. He's romantic.'

I looked her over. Her face was drawn from the last time I had seen her, and there were little puckers around her eyes. She handed me something.

'Did you see it?'

'What is it?'

'The ship's paper.'

'No, I didn't. I guess I'm not interested.'

'It's in there.'

'What's in there?'

'About the wedding. Lola and Nino. It came in by radio a little after noon.'

'Oh, they're married?'

'Yes. It was pretty exciting. Mr Keyes gave her away. They went to San Francisco on their honeymoon. Your company paid Nino a bonus.'

'Oh. It must be out then. About us.'

'Yes. It all came out. It's a good thing we're under different names here. I saw all the passengers reading about it at lunch. It's a sensation.'

'You don't seem worried.'

'I've been thinking about something else.'

She smiled then, the sweetest, saddest smile you ever saw. I thought of the five patients, the three little children, Mrs Nirdlinger, Nirdlinger, and myself. It didn't seem possible that anybody that could be as nice as she was when she wanted to be, could have done those things.

'What were you thinking about?'

'We could be married, Walter.'

'We could be. And then what?'

I don't know how long we sat looking out to sea after that. She started it again. 'There's nothing ahead of us, is there Walter?'

'No. Nothing.'

'I don't even know where we're going. Do you?'

'No.'

'. . . Walter, the time has come.'

'What do you mean, Phyllis?'

'For me to meet my bridegroom. The only one I ever loved. One night I'll drop off the stern of the ship. Then, little by little I'll feel his icy fingers creeping into my heart.'

'. . . I'll give you away.'

'What?'

'I mean: I'll go with you.'

'Its all that's left, isn't it?'

Keyes was right. I had nothing to thank him for. He just saved the state the expense of getting me.

We walked around the ship. A sailor was swabbing out the gutter outside the rail. He was nervous, and caught me looking at him. 'There's a shark. Following the ship.'

I tried not to look, but couldn't help it. I saw a flash of dirty white down in the green. We walked back to the deck chairs.

'Walter, we'll have to wait. Till the moon comes up.'

'I guess we better have a moon.'

'I want to see that fin. That black fin. Cutting the water in the moonlight.'

*

The captain knows us. I could tell by his face when he came out of the radio room a little while ago. It will have to be tonight. He's sure to put a guard on us before he puts into Mazatlan.

The bleeding has started again. The internal bleeding, I mean, from the lung where the bullet grazed it. It's not much but I spit blood. I keep thinking about that shark.

I'm writing this in the stateroom. It's about half past nine. She's in her stateroom getting ready. She's made her face chalk white, with black circles under her eyes and red on her lips and cheeks. She's got that red thing on. It's awful-looking. It's just one big square of red silk that wraps around her, but it's got no armholes, and her hands look like stumps underneath it when she moves them around. She looks like what came aboard the ship to shoot dice for souls in the *Rime of the Ancient Mariner*.

I didn't hear the stateroom door open, but she's beside me now while I'm writing. I can feel her.

The moon.